AF508315

Though this novel does contain documented history, it is a work of fiction. Names, characters, organizations, and events are the product of the author's imagination or are used fictitiously. Any resemblance to actual persons, living or dead, or actual events is purely coincidental.

This book contains graphic scenes, sex, historical recreations, profanity, and topics that may make some people uncomfortable.

Published by The Mighty Phen
Warner Robins, GA

ISBN 979-8-9949714-1-3
Cover design by Phen Rambles
Interior design by Phen Rambles

Originates in the United States of America

First Edition

Between Two Guys

PREFACE

The three eldest Washington children will represent different legacies as they grow older: autonomy; excellence; and authenticity. It does not mean either one is more of that than the other two, though this narrative may imply that statement false about at least one of them, while showing you who potentially embodies all three.

Recognition > Control
Honesty > Need
Presence > Possession

Generally speaking, I think life prepares us for the partners we're supposed to have, not necessarily the partners we end up choosing. The trappings of social media narratives from pseudo-experts; the portrayal of couples working through misunderstandings and mismatches under the fear of being alone; or perceived as unworthy to be coupled... influence how people think relationships actually work, and should work. The question will always be 'why do you have these standards: because that's what you want, or because that's what you are told you should want.'

I was told it is hard to find the joy in my books, which surprises me... because there is absolute joy in every book. There is resiliency; there is success; there is a lack of struggle porn. They are allowed to 'live white' without being white. The joy is in being able to live through the bullshit, grow in spite of the weight on top of your head... and prove to society who the DEI really is. We need these standards against discrimination because YOU can't see the greatness and the competence of Black people... not because we are not great.

Our central love interests are authentically Black in

their portrayal. Lamar is 80s fine. Tall, "cutest guy on JV," and jovial. Great eyes, long eyelashes, just insanely pretty. Think Michael Ealy; Daniel Sunjata; Jesse Williams; Boris Kodjoe. Roman is, coincidentally, a statuesque figure with classically handsome features wrapped in the finest of pure dark cacao. When I envision him, I think of the 90s and figures like Eddie Murphy, Wesley Snipes, Omar Epps, Morris Chestnut.

Marcus is 90s fine, white turtleneck era. Those were his high school and college years, anyway, so he definitely brings that vibe to his children. You can make the argument that his sexual appeal was based on his demographics being popular at the time... although Marcus is independently a beautiful man with an enormous smile; Taye Diggs, for example. His son, Aegan, is arguably the darkest of his children; and narratively, the most attractive in every aspect. Unlike his dad and his older brother, he is intentionally unapproachable, wielding his charm with precision and discernment. He sees the world for what it is, and wants to protect those it wants to harm, including his gay younger brother: Morocco.

Aegan learned a lot of things from the legacy of Eigan and Hanjoon, and that's what this story is kind of about: how children can embody the influences of those who went before them. Sometimes, they do this to bring future generations into the awareness established by those predecessors. As with many children, they "don't want to hear all that" and seek to do their own thing. That's not always a bad thing, but you can appreciate how those who want the legacy to continue will become offended. There is an eventuality where that lesson will force itself to be taught... There's an appreciation that no matter the quality of the vessel, it might not be the vessel that's going to bring you what you need to learn.

Even though Morocco may struggle with being a part of the continuation of the legacy his parents laid down, he will become an exhibition of it nonetheless. It is because of the reception by Denae and Marcus for what they learned from Eigan and Hanjoon, that we don't have to write Morocco as a statistic. Hyun might be the lightest of his brothers, but he still won't pass a paper bag test, so to speak. Him being the brother behind Morocco will become a key later on. We can write them both in complete, pure, Black boy love and joy, and let them live the life of ordinary teenagers, whatever ordinary looks like... because it means different things to different people. I bring this up because the night before I write this preface, one of my associations didn't understand what I meant when I said "I feel like a teenager" while handling the afterglow of a fantastic date. Said associate took the time to talk about how his 'teenage years were horrible.' So were mine... but if we can't dive in to context and realize I'm talking about joys and the 'boy crush' side of teenage life, not the "I'm going to beat your ass because I found out you were telling me the truth" abuse I endured...

I wrote this book because of the craze around a white gay man producing a white woman's M/M romance book about two gay hockey players. So yes, Roman plays hockey on purpose, and I am not shying away from that. What pissed me off more than anything is how, in the online discourse, people were criticizing how the only Black character in the series got a little too close to the neck of the main character... and "how aggressive and non-consensual" that was.

Ok... fair point.

But... in one scene featuring the two white... pardon... one white guy and one half-Asian; half-white guy, the white man was LITERALLY jacking his dick while eyeing the object of his affection in the shower. But that wasn't considered aggressive or non-consensual? Ok. And... according to some people who allegedly read the books, it was a Black man who encouraged at least one of our star hockey players to come out? Interesting, where was he in the series? Oh, he got erased. And, in the book... the half-Asian was actually soliciting advances from the Black guy who almost kissed him on his neck, and breathed... on his neck?

Hmmm.

White gays are never beating the allegations. So even the white woman included the importance of Black men, but the white gay decided "nah, we don't need all that wokeness, how dare Black men be attractive and uplifting"?

CHIIIIIIIIIIIIIIIIIIL'!

And we haven't even touched the "white man able to navigate and be accepted in his whiteness, but he thinks society will harm him like it does 'the Blacks' if he comes out the closet, so he hides" narrative that has been overdone and oft-repeated in movies and books for decades.

Y'all don't get tired of that?

I guess some people like to read about their trauma, too, instead of using medium to portray the kind of world you want to see.

In that spirit... my Black gays are open and out. How they navigate it looks different, but they are not going back into the closet: PERIOD! They may convert to B temporarily while struggling with sexual positions, because too many tops orgasm off the idea of dominating another man as opposed to actually not wanting to bottom. That's probably why some men eventually struggle in the bedroom... because they stifle their own desire in response to what society says a man should look like, and how he should behave... but that is slightly getting off topic.

If this is your first time reading my work, the title has lots of different meanings... it is literal, and it is figurative. The two guys varies... sometimes it is an internal struggle, sometimes it is external. If you have already enjoyed "The Strength that Stayed," yes... this book is based on that short story. It is chronological... so you don't have to worry about when we are talking about the present and when we are talking about the past (the first book in this universe). You may wonder why I leave some details out, but the perspective is from children who did not experience what you can read in the previous two books. I will also add that this is technically the fourth book in the series... but the third book won't write itself, so here we are. The third book dives on the same societal, political, 'here's a history lesson' that 'Security Among Titles' and 'Grown Folks' Business' highlight. 'Between Two Guys' is, hopefully, 99 percent love story and teenage angst.

The sex scenes are narrative, not exploitative. This is not a chance to assume what I am attracted to. The only thing these boys can do for me... is point me to their fathers. But we should not pretend that kids and teens don't have and don't think about sex. I do my best to keep the details as tight as possible, because the narrative is more important than wanton gratuitousness.

I do wish Eigan and Hanjoon could see the beauty of the lives of the Washington Family. I know some of you familiar with this universe are going to be mad about two things that happen later on in the book... but if you understand the legacy of who is affected, you will be happy he is allowed to live a full life, and not become a

history lesson. As far as the second one...
Just read it... and more importantly...

ENJOY!

-Stephen Rambles

INTRODUCTION

From the street, a pristine landscaping scene underlines an immaculate one-story home outside of Sacramento. The serenity on the outside... betrayed by the chaos on the inside.

One boy, Hannon... quietly playing his video games... dressed and ready for an excursion. A second boy runs around the house... naked... giggling and laughing... dodging clothes... and two adults: a nanny, and daddy.

"Aegan... PUT SOME CLOTHES ON NOW!"

A frustrated father trying to surprise his wife, but his little free-spirited one is picking the wrong time to be consistently himself.

"No!"

He squeals... hiding in places that must have appeared out of no where just to conceal him and infuriate his two pursuers.

'Thank God he's potty trained.' The father breathes a sigh of relief before yelling at his son again.

Part of the reason his son "can't" hear him... a third boy... screaming in dad's arms... trying to wrench free and run around with his brother.

"Down..." Morocco cries... "DOOOOOOWWWN!"

He longs to be free and run like Aegan, who likes to show off for his little brother... but Morocco is already clothed. All three of them should have been clothed... but 'that damn Aegan!'

Defiant. He let the doctors know he was in the womb on his own time... he let the world know he was coming on his own time... and he has never known what restraint means.

"Morocco, please!"

Pointless requests from daddy to son. Almost regretting his libido... but in the quiet times... whenever they are... he is always ready to make another one.

Hannon is no help at all, but at least he isn't causing any trouble. He learned early about his brother Aegan. Morocco and any additional children might give in to his status as oldest... but not that one.

Marcus sits down with Morocco, almost willing to surrender... when all of a sudden... a little naked body plops down on the floor, feet away from where Hannon mimics the sounds of his video game, and begins to snore. Marcus relaxes just enough, now weak... to allow tear-soaked Morocco to squirm from his hands and go lay next to his brother. He keeps his clothes on, thankfully, and falls asleep, too. The nanny, still searching for Aegan in other parts of the house... but Marcus is too tired to inform her of the scene. Silence will let her know. He closes his eyes... just as the front door opens.

"This place looks like HELL!"

Denae was expecting an anniversary outing with her most favorite boys in the world.

She only has a brief break before she has to return to the station for the late night news. She turns the corner to see her husband... exhausted... Hannon "pew-pew"ing with his video game... and...

"Them two right there!" She smirks.

Now is probably not the best time to tell Marcus he did it again.

Eigan comes in the door...

"Con-gra-tu-LA-A-A-A-SHUNS!" He sings.

"Gon' somewhere with that noise!" Marcus yells in his sleep.

** * * * **

Instead of going out, a few friends and family from out of town come over to the house, Overstimulated by guests, the boys run around and play... yes, Aegan has his clothes on.

He hears a familiar cry behind him... and runs inside.

He sees his brother being held by... who cares?
"You not holding him right!"
Aegan hits the adult.
"Give me my brother!" He demands.
Hanjoon Jee, done for the evening at the station, yells from across the room...
"Aegan Ivey!"
is not going to remove the grimace from Aegan's face.

Obediently, the adult puts Morocco on the ground. Aegan grabs Morocco's hand and takes him outside.

** * * * **

Living in Chicago, is a little different from the Central Valley. Aegan misses life near the coast, but few things are better than being close to U-town and going down with dad; Eigan and Hanjoon to watch rugby games. Hannon gets to work the sidelines a little bit, playing with the ball, setting up the gear. The three boys can't wait to run with the bison. Their dad played here, Eigan played here... a strong legacy has been established and Hannon can't wait to be the first to add to it.

Aegan clings to Hanjoon; his dad was quite adamant today about him behaving... not that he cares... 'Aegan gon' be Aegan.' His little shadow, Morocco, clings to him. Aegan and Morocco are practically inseparable as they grow up.

"That's gon' be us, Roc."

Aegan points to the field. Morocco nods in agreement. Marcus cannot help but be proud of his sons. They never get on his nerves, relatively speaking.

Aegan is a great brother to follow. There is not an award he won't win in any sport he plays; or a problem he can't solve in any field of academia... at least so far at the prep school level. He was raised on a standard of how to excel; so that when Morocco comes along, he has something to be better than. He loves his brother, and can't wait for him to blossom into his potential.

On any random day, them two will fight each other... Morocco will lose and go crying for protection. Then run right back to lay with his brother like nothing happened. They easily forget a lot about each other, around each other. They just love each other's energy.

On a rare day, mom and dad take their younger brothers and grandmother away... leaving the three boys alone in the house... for logistics' sake. Hannon takes the time to sneak a girl into his grandmother's room... since he's not bold enough to take her all the way upstairs to his room. Morocco, who had been asleep, sneaks around the corner... stares at his brother... who looks back at him... then proceeds. Morocco runs back downstairs.

"Guess what Hannon's doing?"

"I don't care," Aegan yawns.

"But he's got—"

"I don't want to fucking know! You know if mom asks me, I'm going to tell her. So don't tell me any damn thing!"

Aegan turns over. Morocco lays back down on his brother... keeping Hannon's secret.

* * * * *

Morocco chirps on about his classes. And some of the fascinating students he learns around. All he does is talk Aegan's ear off.

"Hey..."

He wants to tell his brother about one particular student...

"You never bring anyone home. How come?"

"Cause I am fine as I am"

Aegan isn't sure how to answer that question anyway.

"Hannon brings home girls... you don't bring home anyone."

"I am fine... as I am."

Aegan repeats, annoyed; concentrating on a crossword.

"Well, what if I bring a girl home?"

"GIRL?! Quit playing!"

"I'm serious... what if I bring a girl... or a guy home?" *Morocco inquires.*

"A guy is more likely," Aegan dismisses the question.

Morocco punches him, starting a fight he cannot win, as Aegan quickly gets the advantage. Morocco escapes and runs upstairs.

"MOOOOM! Aegan is picking on me!"

"Yeah... cause he talking about bringing boys home; and there's enough sex in this house as it is."

Aegan defends himself.

"Watch your mouth, Aegan!"

Denae knows her and Marcus aren't exactly discreet and that better be who Aegan is talking about because she knows Hannon better not be–

She pauses.

Aegan and Morocco freeze... mouths slowly opening... eyes widening. Aegan's "oh shit" meter spins out of control.

Denae yells to Marcus...

"Your son just outed his brother!"

"AEGAN?!"

Marcus summons his son... who doesn't move.

"I don't hear feet!"

Aegan smirks; then winks at Morocco, who begins to cry as Aegan heads upstairs. Not for being outed, but because Aegan is in serious trouble now.

"Oh, Morocco... who is he?!"

Denae embraces her son. He's going to tell Aegan first, who does she think she is?

About twenty minutes later, Aegan... back downstairs... Morocco jumps on top of him to lay down.

"Get the fuck off of me!"

Aegan yells, but he's not going to push Morocco away. And Morocco knows that.

"You want round two?" Marcus booms.

"No sir!"

Aegan falls asleep with Morocco snoring on him.

All it takes is one moment, paying attention to what everyone else believes is the wrong thing, because the universe forces your gaze to view it.

Four family members leave Daddy Halsted's, heading to the biggest game in town...

Lamar Barnes attends a performing arts school, Sable; a few blocks away from The Academy. He doesn't want to completely abandon his love for "sportsball," as some of his schoolmates call it. There's nothing wrong with their kind of gay, it's just not his kind of gay. How fortunate that Sable has a partnership with The Academy to give students a complete selection of athletic outlets, if they so seek one. Besides, he's not fully out just yet: still getting courted by the girls at Sable... still being teased like he's one of the "bruhs" at Academy. Maybe it's safety, maybe it's puberty.

It's not unheard of for a JV player to dunk, especially at this school. The Academy has been sending All-Americans to blue-blood basketball schools and the pros for a few years now, churning out state championships in the interim. In fact, one of those all-star alum is in the building tonight. 'I guess Dear, Old U is on a bye?' Lamar hasn't been checking the schedule this season, worried about his own commitments in dance; orchestra; art; and basketball.

He knows the crowd isn't here to cheer JV on: they want to get good seats before varsity takes the court in the biggest rivalry game every year for The Academy, especially the past couple of seasons; and possibly get a glimpse of Hannon Washington, who's having a decent season in college. "Dear, Old U" might actually win it all, cause their roster is loaded!

JV is against a lesser opponent, but still an important game on the schedule. A few school scouts in the audience, so there's a little more showboating than usual... to which Lamar won't be left out.

Less than a minute left... seconds ticking away... down by one... the offense is playing keep away with four up top. He has to time it just right...

"BARNES WITH THE STEAL..." as the crowd erupts.

Not sure if it's the takeaway or something else responsible for the ruckus, Lamar dribbles past half court... unstoppable... untouchable...

Hannon walks in... time to impress... but something distracts Lamar, and he hangs on the rim just a little too long... needing his shooting arm to break his fall.

"Technical foul... 1+1, black team..." as Lamar writhes in a bit of pain, suppressing it because he doesn't want to 'seem like a punk.' He limps over to the bench, assisted by a few coaches.

"At least you made the shot, are you ok?" Hannon inquires. Lamar looks right past him, and smiles...

"Yeah, I'm alright," as his eyes glisten at Hannon's shadow... who cannot help but feel smitten, as the shadow tries to hide behind his brother.

Hannon picks up on the cue, and turns to Joey Parker... "Go sit down somewhere!"

"Um... he's not looking at me," Joey corrects the assumption.

Hannon, confused, feels a pull on his jacket, as his brother peeks from behind him.

"Hi, I'm Lamar..."

as he shakes Hannon's hand... still looking at the curious little first-year clinging to the basketball phenom, pretending to be shy.

"Hi, Lamar," Hannon hears from behind him.

Not sure how to react to this situation, Hannon turns and pulls his brother away... as they head to find some empty seats in the stands... greeting unfamiliar faces that recognize Hannon Washington. Lamar follows with his eyes as much as he can... ignoring the groan from the crowd at the results of the game.

Lamar can't keep his mind off of what he just saw, not even the pain in his arm or the crack in his heel can put his mind back on the game. He remains seated on the bench, nursing his wounds, trying to hide his body's response to what he just observed from the hardcourt.

"You staying to watch varsity?"

The boys ask each other while showering and changing clothes. Robert eases over to Lamar.

"Dude... I can understand being starstruck, but what the hell was that with Hannon?"

"You ever looked at someone, and... just knew there was something special about them?"

Robert pauses...

"Well, that's how friendships are made, but the way you were looking at him... Look, we all know you go to Sable: it's cool. Not everyone over there is queer, but we don't really put up with that gay shit over here, man. I'm not going to tell anyone, just keep that shit to yourself if you're going to be on this team."

"Man, quit trolling; I wasn't even looking at him like that."

Lamar has no idea what Robert is talking about... not even willing to form a better response. He's not sure what's going on, he only knows he just became curious about someone. Varsity players file back into the locker room from warm-ups, as coach gives a pre-game speech...

"And we have a surprise guest..." as if everyone doesn't know who it is.

Hannon enters, followed by Aegan, who is obviously just here because his brother's in town... and then the boy still clinging to Hannon. Lamar can't keep his eyes off of him... and the boy seems to be just as curious, poorly hiding his coyness. It makes a few of the players a bit uneasy, cause 'that's definitely a fag'... but there are two reasons no one will make a scene... one of them much more deadly than the other.

Robert now realizes who Lamar is talking about... whispers...

"I'd stay away from that one... Aegan don't play about his brother."

Since Lamar isn't a student at The Academy, he is not aware of the hierarchy. The only reason he knows of Aegan is because he's principal trumpet in the community youth orchestra; didn't know he was related to Hannon, let alone that they have a younger brother.

"What you mean?"

"Aegan is a fucking bully, man. He pops off quick. He runs a few clubs around here, really protects the alphabet people. Bitch think he's an activist or something, trying to save the whole fucking world. He lucky he don't get caught outside slipping."

"You'd shoot him?"

"Nah, not me... but someone might. He go out like his gay ass uncles."

Robert mimics firing a gun.

"He must have kicked your ass," Lamar correctly assesses. "Just take the L, man. Nothing wrong with that."

"Shut yo' gay ass up!"

"Is there something more important than what we have going on, Moore and Barnes?" Coach chastises.

The two boys hush. Aegan's brother covers his mouth, hiding a laugh. Lamar smirks back, bowing his head to pretend being ashamed.

Had Lamar been paying attention, he would have heard the name of his new crush... but now, those details will be postponed.

* * * * *

The universe gives you the information you need... on its time, not your own; but there is something to be said for a little proactive behavior to nudge things along.

Lamar heads over to practice a little early today.

He's been doing that for a few weeks, ever since he saw... him. Unanswered friend requests to Hannon and Aegan have put his 'missing persons' search on hold. And Robert isn't really giving him much information.

"I don't know them like that. He's a senior."

Aegan and a few guys are leaving the weight room in the gym. Lamar makes a move...

"I didn't know you play ball, too?"

"I don't, that's Hannon's field of expertise."

Aegan slows down, turns... nodding the other guys ahead.

"Oh... so who you working out with?"

"Rugby season's restarting soon. It's going to be rough year... if you must know."

Lamar isn't picking up on the 'get the fuck away from me cues.' Aegan isn't as offputting as rumored.

"Nice... I don't really know anything about that sport."

"You go to Sable, right? A few of our teammates go there."

"How you know I go to Sable?"

"You play on the basketball team and keep eyeing my brother every time we go to a game. You either want to fuck him, or get fucked up... I got time either way."

Lamar gets a taste of whether or not Robert was telling the truth.

"Damn, you a mean fuck!"

"Thanks for the compliment."

Aegan begins to walk off.

"So... no, I don't want to fuck your brother. But... I do at least want to know his name. He's got a look about him... I don't know. Like, I don't think I'm gay, but... it's just something about him."

Aegan pauses.

"My brother is not allowed to date. He's still figuring out some things himself... but he is absolutely and unapologetically gay; of that, he is very sure. He knows who you are... what do you want me to tell him?"

"Tell him he made me hurt my arm"

Lamar attempts levity... with no smile from Aegan.

"Oh... um..." Lamar adjusts... uncomfortably awkward.

Aegan turns and walks off... laughing disrespectfully at this poor attempt to impress.

'Damn, he IS a bitch.'

Lamar pulls out his phone... to delete his friend requests to Hannon and Aegan. The little he can see, Aegan doesn't post much about his family anyway; plenty of activist posts. And Hannon's page is a highlight reel. The only other Washingtons on both their pages appear to be cousins who don't even live here. 'Maybe their brother doesn't have any social media.' His friend circle doesn't really overlap with many kids at The Academy, so he has to put his search on hold for the moment. It's not worth the humiliation.

* * * * *

Denae ignores the boys fighting downstairs. It's too early in the evening for this foolishness. Marcus will be home soon anyway... he can take care of it.

The front door slams shut.

Angry feet storm upstairs.

"Put a hole in my floor if you want to..."

as she turns the page in the paper. Aegan, slamming kitchen cabinets.

"Why does he hate me so damn much? All the shit I do for him!"

"He doesn't hate you, he just thinks you're performative. He's still working through some things, Aegan... you know that."

"He don't need to be dating anyone right now... he just started at Academy, doesn't he know the legacy there?"

Denae turns the page again.

"That's part of the problem."

"I just want him to be good, ma... there's nothing wrong with that."

"Stop pressuring that boy... being good won't keep the homophobes away."

"I know... but that's not the point." Aegan munches.

Denae peruses the back page of the paper.

"Where's he going?"

"I don't know... probably to see if he can get to basketball practice before it ends."

Aegan grabs a few snacks and storms up to his room.

"Aegan... you cannot save everyone. You also cannot control everyone. It's not going to change what happened to Eigan and Hanjoon. You need to learn how to live... and let live."

He pauses on the stairs.

"I'm not trying to control him! Why can't anyone see me the way they see Hannon? And now I'm getting skipped over!"

"Aegan, everyone sees you. You are just unsure of what they see about you... so that's why you feel ignored. You're reliable, and most people want to feel needed. You're not looking for that, you're looking for someone who is already whole, and growing in their completeness... able to break into new ventures by choice... not by force. You, unfortunately or fortunately, learned how to do that young. Let everyone else develop at their own pace."

"Whatever..."

"Don't 'whatever' me, boy... as if I don't know what I'm talking about. You always do that when someone has you pegged. You're very grounded, son. People run from you because they don't know how to do that yet. In a world of uncertainty: you're solid... and that makes you stand out... makes you unapproachable. You know who you're named after," Denae smiles.

"I feel like I am nothing like him, though.
Hanjoon and I resonated–"

"Yeah, but Hanjoon was the quiet one. I'll
admit you share his ability to lead and guide,
though."

"Then why won't that damn son of yours
listen!"

Aegan slams the door to his room...

"I just know that boy don' lost his mind!"

Marcus enters the home, heading upstairs... as
Denae continues reading.

* * * * *

Lamar heads out the back of the gym. Practice was
exhausting today. He feels defeated in so many
ways. He takes his time heading out the locker
room... he's going to miss his bus... which means he
will get to the train late as well. Maybe his mom put
some money on his card so he can do a rideshare...
he really doesn't want to be around people today.

Feeling betrayed by his teammates as Robert, failing
to keep his promise, began the whispers of his
attraction to Aegan's brother. It's confusing,
because Lamar isn't even sure of what's going on
with him right now... so how can everyone else be
so adamant, and punish him for their assumptions.

He sits outside the gym... just inside of the back
steps to the parking lot. The janitor ignores him for
the moment, since there are still a few other teams
inside practicing. He puts his head back and drifts
away.

For whatever reason, he dreams, in this brief moment, that Aegan relays his message... and then, white wedding bells. He smiles in his slumber.

"Is your arm better?"

Lamar hears in his dream, but ignores answering it.

He feels someone sit next to him, but that's not what's happening in his dream... it wakes him up. A girl is sitting by his side.

"You don't go to Academy, do you?" She asks.

"No, I go to Sable."

"Oh... well, you're really cute... can I get your number or your page?"

Lamar pulls out his phone to enter in her number. Surprised at how bold she is, he smiles. They both turn as someone clamors up the back stairs... and in walks...

"Morocco, what are you doing here so late?" The girl asks.

He stares at Lamar... confused. She turns back to see Lamar has stood up... and is staring at Morocco. She slowly rises... without being noticed... and walks down the hall in despair.

Lamar takes a step towards Morocco... who is still very confused. 'Did he misread the signs? Is he about to have to defend himself? Why is Lamar just staring at him like this?' For weeks, he wondered what this moment would look like... and now that it's here... he should just turn and run away... 'Lamar likes girls.'

"A beautiful name for a beautiful boy…"

is all that he hears… freezing him in his retreat.
Lamar walks up behind him, and embraces his waist.

"I've been looking for you…"

Lamar whispers into the wavy strands of Morocco's
mane.

He reaches behind him… to caress the face he has
been dreaming about. Lamar turns him around…
and kisses him on his lips.

Morocco pushes away…

"Don't you know any damn thing about
consent?"

And runs out the back door of the gym. Lamar just
stands there… in awe… absorbing that first touch.

"I'm going to marry that boy."

Mother Washington decided the family needed a big meal tonight, so there's much more food than usual. Aegan, already on his second plate... endured his punishment from Marcus, apologizing to his mom just in time... because grand-grand made his favorite dessert: lemon meringue!

How she can hide food in that house from this scavenger should be studied... but this isn't her first time protecting food from growing teenage boys.

The front door opens... Denae places a hand on Marcus. He huffs and puffs... wanting to do something, but knowing he won't make it past the two women in the house to do anything.

"I'm going to my den."

He heads upstairs with a plate of food.

Morocco comes upstairs... all smiles... and pecks Aegan on his forehead.

"Man, get the fuck away from me!"

Aegan winces as soon as the words leave his mouth. Denae pretends to be deaf... though Mother Washington does not.

"Watch yo' mouth at this table, your dad need to come back down?"

"Ya'll always take his side!"

Aegan swallows his food, as his other brothers laugh at him getting in trouble.

"You 'posed to be eating," he scolds... to which silverware returns to being scraped across plates.

"You like to feel needed, just admit it"

Denae wipes the messy mouths and fingers of the youngest.

"Nah... just like for people to pretend they know better."

Aegan finishes his plate and goes upstairs.

Morocco kisses his grandmother... and follows Aegan upstairs with a plate.

"Them two are ridiculous," Denae and Mother Washington laugh.

As Aegan tries to work on a major writing project...

"And then I get there... and he's all nestled up to some girl. So I'm like, confused and everything... but I just stand there."

"Who was it?"

"Maryann, on the booster squad. Cutest boy on JV looking at me... she couldn't stand it," Morocco laughs.

"So... then what happened?"

"Then... this boy come up to me grabbing and kissing me. So, I let him feel me up a little bit," Morocco giggles.

"You damn whore, I told you about that."

"I know... but that felt good as fuck... chil'... I almost lost it. But then I yelled at him for not consenting and ran off."

Morocco feels proud. Aegan turns irate.

"Why would you do that?"

"Huh? He supposed to ask before he does that! Aint' no rape culture 'round here. One hundred percent consent... on god. These men already acting grown... isn't that what you warned me about?"

"Yeah, but not if you like him. Now the boy confused... he gon' think both of us mean as hell... and you don't have the resume I do. Why even tell you just for you to pull some crap like that... damn: you dumb as hell! Now he probably gon' go around beating up gays because you did that. Selfish ass!"

Aegan scolds as he continues typing.

"You take that back! I'm not fucking selfish!"

Morocco throws some food at Aegan, but misses and hits one of his posters. Aegan stops typing.

"MOOOOOOOOOOOOM!"

Morocco runs out of the room. Marcus peeks in...

"I swear... you two need to figure it the fuck out! I get tired of this arguing shit every damn night. That's your brother... not your sister. You won't be able to manhandle him for long."

"You still manhandle your siblings," Aegan murmurs.

"Keep talking... you gon' get what you asked for."

Aegan sucks his teeth... "Look what he did to my poster! And then he leaves his damn plate in here!"

Marcus stares at his son... who rolls his eyes...

"I'll roll 'em back!"

Marcus corrects... as Aegan takes the plate downstairs.

"MOROCCO!"

who comes upstairs with a rag to clean up his mess, sheepish around Marcus.

Downstairs in the kitchen...

"Ugh... he likes Lamar even more now," Aegan tells his mother and grandmother.

"We know," they both bemoan.

First time in a long time this house will have to deal with teenage love woes... cause it seems like the universe wants Morocco to date.

Lamar enters his home, on a high. His mom's not back from work yet... so he has the place to himself. He definitely needs some alone time... cause that was intense. He takes a box of tissues to his room.

"WOW..." is about all he can manage to say.

This might be a multi-session, cause it's not going down any time soon. He got to smell him... hear him... taste him... touch him... the other four senses now understanding the mystery that is—

"Morocco!"

He yells... as keys jingle at the front door. He shuffles to clean himself up.

"Who is Morocco? And why are you yelling names?"

Dr. Barnes takes her coat off, getting home a little earlier than expected... so subsequent rounds will definitely have to wait. Lamar shuffles out the back bedroom.

"Um... ma? We've never really talked about this, but I think I like dudes"

Lamar feels empowered to say it for some reason, still caught up in the euphoria of the evening.

His mother quietly heads over to the recliner... and turns on the TV. Lamar, unsure of what this response means, tries to hide without moving. It's something that has been churning in his mind for weeks. He always knew he would say it... but the plans rarely manifest themselves the way you hope. A tear rolls down his mother's face.

"Being black isn't difficult enough, Lamar?"

"I don't know, ma; I'm too young to understand some things–"

"Exactly!"

"But I know I like this guy, and I wasn't sure until today... when I touched him... and kissed him–"

"Oh, damn... so we ordered the express package to hell, huh?"

"Ma... I can't think that love like this would send me to hell. God can't be in the business of punishing this... I don't know. Touching him felt so natural for me, like I have been waiting for him or something like that. I don't know," Lamar reasons.

"You really like him, huh?" Dr. Barnes stares at the TV.

"So far... he got mad at me already, though," Lamar bows his head.

"Already? Well goddamn! What happened?"

Dr. Barnes, not sure how she is supposed to respond, loves her son. 'His sins are between him and God, just like mine are between me and God.'

"He says I don't know about consent. I couldn't help myself, I want him."

Dr. Barnes reflects a bit...

"First, I'm sorry for reacting how I did. It's a reflex, not an excuse... but we are just conditioned to respond to certain news in certain ways. Does he make you happy?"

"I don't know, we haven't really been around

each other, he doesn't have any social media. I don't know how I am going to get in touch with him. He has this pissant for a brother... and that's putting it nicely."

Lamar slightly balls a fist.

"Well... are you dating him or his brother?"

Lamar pauses for a moment...

"But what if his family doesn't like me?"

"Are you dating him, or his family?"

Lamar is unsure what the answer is.

"Not even every straight couple has the permission of their parents to be together, but your parents are not in your relationship... or at least, they shouldn't be. What's his name, Morocco...?"

"Washington," Lamar sighs in admiration.

"Hmmm... that name sounds familiar for some reason. He came over to the school earlier today... looking for you. I guess now I know why. Seems like you both were looking for each other for a while, and it culminated today. No way that boy would run from Academy to Sable and back if he wasn't desperate," she considers.

"Wait... so you knew this whole time? You think he likes me?!"

"Well, I wasn't sure that you were gay... but yes, I knew he was looking for you today. I wasn't going to say anything. But there must be something here, son. I can work on me...

but the happiest times in my life were with your dad. I couldn't imagine anyone telling me that we shouldn't be together."

Dr. Barnes' tears betray her support. She can't help thinking about HIV, and can't help thinking about prostitutes and child trafficking. Her mind races, but Lamar does not see the confusion on her face as he hugs her.

"I love you, mom."

"What the hell you doing here, fresh-fag?"

A few of the JV players tease Morocco, who has been showing up to watch practice and maybe get to know Lamar a little better. He ignores the jeers, he and Denae just had a mani-pedi day and he is not trying to mess up his nails... just yet.

"La-Mary isn't on the team anymore, he dropped out," the boys laugh.

To hell with his nails.

Three boys tried to subdue Morocco, but one got bitten; one got severely scratched... and the third got the message. He's learned more from his brother than has been rumored. And they don't even know who his boxing coach is. Nonetheless, you always keep them guessing... never let them know you have training.

"Break it up!" Coach yells at the players...

"We don't do that here! It's bad enough we're down a player... and y'all got the nerve to be fighting! As if we can afford a suspension right now!"

The end of the JV season is almost here, but a few of the JV squad also play varsity, so he needs ballers to be available... not kicked off for bullying.

"You know what to do... seems like you have plenty of energy today!"

He blows his whistle twice... as players moan and groan through suicides. Coach turns to Morocco.

"You're looking for Lamar? He said he wanted to quit the team. Not sure what prompted it, though," Coach informs.

Morocco, feeling a bit guilty, thanks coach for the information.

"Hey... not all of us care about him being gay, or you being gay. You trying out for the baseball team this year, aren't you?"

Coach has been scouting Morocco since his middle school days.

"Yes. But, I also need to fulfill my dance commitments"

Morocco turns to walk away.

"Well, I get along pretty well with the dance teacher, so we can work around that schedule," Coach coaxes.

"I'm thinking about enrolling at Sable," Morocco corrects.

"Oh... well, why not here?"

"Because here... there's too much legacy to follow. I need to make sure people like me for me... and not for what my brothers have done."

"But you're in a completely different sport?"

"Aegan is my brother. Sports is not the only place where we overlap. His name is every where... including the dance program here! And I don't want to get a fighting reputation either..."

Morocco gives more of an explanation than needed.

Coach laughs.

"Yeah, he's going to leave a lasting impression. But I get the feeling you will be respected in

your own right. Sable has a good program,
need a recommendation?"

Aegan, leaving the practice fields, heads into the
gym... sees Morocco talking with coach.

"You ready to go?" he yells.

Morocco runs off... heading to his brother's side.

"He quit the team," he cries once they get in
the car.

Aegan presses the clutch; puts the car in gear; and
drives out the parking lot, without responding.
Caught up in the loyalty that his brother gives him,
Morocco relies on the ever-presence of Aegan...
without the requirement of reciprocation.

Even though it's a few years later, it's a much quieter
transition to graduation for Aegan than with
Hannon. No TV cameras camped out at the house;
no coaches visiting all the time. It's kind of
refreshing. For all the greatness that Aegan
displays, Morocco believes no one knows who his
brother is. He revels in what he believes is forced
humility on Aegan.

It's not that Morocco wants his brother to fail, he
just hates how impenetrable he appears to be. He
can't beat him in sports; isn't smarter than he is;
can't beat him in a fight... no one in school has been
able to. He's a superman... and he is always going to
be around, so Morocco can dismiss him, while
relying on his immortality.

Aegan breaks his silence.

"You coming to my game this weekend,
right?"

Morocco pauses...

"I don't like your teammates."

"This is a big game, you always like to watch me play–"

"Well, I don't want to this week! You're going to do fine, you always do fine. You got all the awards in the world... is that not enough? Why do you need me there?"

"Need and want are not the same thing. You already missed my concert, you already missed so much. You think I care about the awards?"

"I know you care about the awards."

Morocco rolls his eyes, looking out the window.

"You're so full of yourself, other people have lives, too."

Aegan shuts down.

He puts the car in park behind the house, but leaves it running. Morocco gets out the car... slamming the door. Aegan allows it... and speeds off down the alley... surprising Morocco.

"Where is he going?"

Morocco sits outside for a bit, waiting for Aegan to come back. It's rare that Aegan just disappears without Morocco being allowed to tag along.

"He's so fucking selfish!"

Morocco storms upstairs... his after school snack waiting for him.

"Your mom is out of town on an assignment. She wants you to call her as soon as possible. Where is Aegan?"

Mother Washington straightens up a few things, preparing for the younger kids to come home from school.

"Being selfish, as usual. Everything is about him!"

"What are y'all fighting about now?"

"I can't miss one damn game without him catching feelings about it. I am allowed to have my own life!"

Morocco moves his food around on the plate.

"He never missed Hannon's games unless he had his own. He's going to be on TV this weekend. It's important to him."

"Oh... so now he think he Hannon or something?"

It's not accurate to say that Morocco is jealous... he is just tired of hearing about things he never really hears about. It makes sense to him... because he replays their accomplishments in his mind, feeling like he hasn't done anything worth overshadowing what his two predecessors have done.

"You're the one who chose to not play baseball this year. I get it, you want to live your own life, but Aegan is not going to always be around."

Mother Washington puts some foil over Aegan's plate as the younger brothers file in the home.

"Lies... Aegan ain't going no where. He loves us all; he loves Chicago. He wouldn't just up and leave."

"All that may be true; but it doesn't mean you can just treat him any kind of way just 'cause you know he can handle it, either."

Morocco snatches his plate and heads outside, as his younger brothers run upstairs, hearing their dad arrive... tackling him... or trying to... as he sees a plate of untouched food.

"Aegan's car isn't here... you know where he is?"

Marcus, tosses his sons around.

"Leave him alone."

Mother Washington hands her son a different plate.

"And Morocco isn't with him?"

"Morocco is still mad about that Lamar boy not being around. He's just trying to show a little independence from his mom and two dads."

"Ugh, I wish Eigan were still around. I don't know how to handle raising this boy, he's so different from Hannon and Aegan... in many ways. Heck, he's different from himself."

"He's going through puberty, but also living in a world that might not accept everything he is the way his family accepts it all. He's going to figure it out."

Mother Washington motions for the boys to eat.

"That's not what I am worried about. What he

will lose in the process is what concerns me."

Marcus continues playing with the boys... ignoring their grandmother for a moment more.

Morocco reenters the home.

"I want to go to dance school," he demands.

"Absolutely not. You're going to Academy, same as your brothers. You had a good year, so what's the problem?"

"I'm not like everyone else, dad. Stop trying to treat me like I am."

"What is this really about? No one in this house has ever tried to make you like anyone else."

"Not all boys play sports, dad."

"There's nothing wrong with sports, Morocco. And you're good at sports, as well as other things."

"I don't want to do sports... or camping... or fix cars... or all that other stuff. I just want to get through school, marry the man of my dreams... and disappear! None of you around here know what it's like to be me and feel so abnormal while doing so-called normal things!"

"All this because you don't want to compete with Aegan and Hannon, huh?"

"There is no competition. I am me... and they are them."

His younger brothers stand aside, waiting for their dad's response. Marcus gets up, staring at his son...

who is waiting to pretend he can beat his dad up. Marcus won't give him the satisfaction of a physical response... not yet anyway.

He's not prepared to deal with his wife if that happens.

* * * * *

Aegan gets back home well after dinner. He and some teammates hung out all afternoon. He opens the door to his room. On his bed is his mail.

His parents let him apply anywhere he wanted to, and he's still receiving interest letters from many schools. He adds to the pile from others that have come before, and opens his letters of acceptance from many schools. He wasn't ready to decide, but it is practically made for him. He borderline understands Morocco's divergence. His parents know he is too free of a spirit; too traveled; too learned; and even though Chicago has personality, she is no longer foreign. He needs something familiar, but with some mystery.

"I guess I've made my decision."

He signs one acceptance letter, putting it in an envelope and taking it downstairs to give to his grandmother... along with a video tape.

"No surprise here," she comments.

Her and the mail carrier will have a lot to talk about on his route tomorrow. Mother Washington gets a rare display of emotion from Aegan.

"I don't care what you say... he hates me for being who I am. Why would he and Hannon do this behind my back? I would have supported anything Roc does. Why shouldn't I feel betrayed?"

He thinks about Morocco enrolling at Sable, with Hannon's help.

"Why should you feel betrayed?"

Aegan's not sure why. He knows Morocco is reaching rebellion age, but why against him? He's always been on his side. He learned as much as he could about everything, and now it just feels like no one needs him at all: not as a source of strength, nor as a bar to surpass... so what was the purpose of being the best? Of being open-minded?

"I guess there's a bit of freedom in him not needing me," Aegan reasons.

"Exactly. You get a chance to live a little. You've never really done that since you came into the world. You spent so much of your life chasing and fighting everyone else, or being chased, that you never really stopped to appreciate what you've built... always making sure everyone else has their bricks because you know you can build without any."

"That's what everyone thinks of me?"

"Aegan Ivey... of course that's what they think of you... you're just too humble to recognize it. And as soon as everyone else is almost finished with their walls, they look over at you... already done... waiting for them to finish, and being honestly happy when they do," she laughs.

"You don't even realize there is a competition:

you trying to make sure everyone eats. And that's a special quality... a rare quality."

Mother Washington turns down the volume on the video they are watching, featuring some of Hanjoon's time playing in college.

"Hanjoon was good at everything he did, too. But he wanted other people to find their light. That's why you identify with him so well."

"They were too young to know them..." Aegan sniffles.

"And there's nothing you can do about that. Hannon had to learn that, too. Morocco gon' be alright. He listens to everything you tell him, you just don't trust that he does."

Mother Washington caresses Aegan's hair.

"Ooo, you need a touch up!"

"Morocco went to the salon by himself. I'm not in the mood to be pretty."

"Boy, we need to take you to the doctor... 'cause I know you fucking lying!"

Mother Washington tickles her grandson.

The Sable School of Performing Arts has seen its share of caliber graduates in theatre, music, dance... Morocco Washington hoping to add his name to the list. Jazz and tap... a sharp contrast to 'backs left' and 'joining the line' for him to defend on plays he has long forgotten, calls he no longer cares to remember.

The bar was set too high, too perfect of a specimen to emulate. He had to form his own path.

New acceptance orientation at Sable, and Aegan refuses to be in attendance. He feels insulted that Morocco chose a different path, now stealing a bit of Aegan's earned spotlight.

"But dance, Morocco?"

Marcus rolls his eyes, still unsure of this... hoping to at least have another math whiz in the family, even without the athletics.

"You'll be alright."

Morocco and his parents walk around to the entrance of the school.

"Where does he get this behavior from? You allow this!" Marcus questions Denae.

They both know where he gets his source of confidence... from his "three parents."

How Aegan speaks to his brothers mirrors their dad... which is probably why Marcus feels the need to rein him in sometimes. Aegan is better than Marcus was in everything; and where they overlap, better than Hannon. He is tall and strong, though he does not always exhaust his strength... at least not for anything anyone knows about.

Yes, Aegan beats up bullies; he has always been that way; but that protection has almost hindered Morocco's growth. He wants to learn that he too can beat up bullies, and not just in the occasional meeting... but every day, if possible. That's some of the inspiration behind this enrollment.

He admires his brother, but his brother is so complete... and it makes Morocco feel inadequate, though Aegan has never belittled his abilities. Perhaps, away from legacy, he will shine without threat of not living up.

"Morocco, you know your dad loves you... he just wants a carbon copy of himself... like his other 2 boys."

Denae kids her husband... who sucks his teeth... long and hard.

"Yeah, well... you better be the best damn dancer they got!" Marcus challenges.

As they enter the school, they are given their tour assignments. But first...

"The headmaster would like to meet you before we do that."

One of the orientation leaders guides the Washingtons to the front office. Dr. Barnes comes from around the corner.

"Good morning, we cannot wait to see you in the fall! I am excited for what you bring to the table, Morocco. I have heard many great things: you come with high praise. Your grades are towards the top of the class... and that is expected to remain consistent during your time here. Also... I have to give full disclosure to you all."

They head in to her office. Denae raises an eyebrow.

"Full disclosure? There shouldn't be any conflicts of interest: he doesn't know anyone here!"

"That's not exactly true. I have been hearing this name for a few weeks now... and it appears you have not made the connection, but I am Lamar's mother."

Denae and Marcus look at each other... and then they both look at Morocco.

"I could have sworn Aegan told you—"

"You!... were supposed to tell us," Denae chides.

"To be fair, I did not know his mom was headmaster," Morocco poorly hides a grin.

Marcus laughs... cause now Denae is caught offguard by her son's antics.

"If it's any consolation, his coach at The Academy told Lamar once we accepted Morocco. But, I also get the feeling Morocco is here to learn. I have seen some of his tapes. And he did state that he always considered Sable, but was told to try The Academy first."

"That's true. Aegan followed Hannon, and they built a strong legacy they were proud to pass to Morocco. Both of them wanted the Washington name over everything; but they love their brother. Besides, there's a few more behind him," Marcus explains.

Morocco rolls his eyes.

"Well... things happen the way they're supposed to happen. I will release you to your guide. Feel free to call me if you have any questions. We should do a dinner or something once the school year ends."

Dr. Barnes releases the family. As the Washingtons leave the office, their guide greets them...

"Hi, my name is Lamar Barnes..."

He smiles... staring at Morocco.

"Welcome to the Sable School of Performing Arts."

Morocco beams! Denae whispers to Marcus...

"Why do I get the feeling you know more about this than you're letting on?"

Marcus grins in his typical Cheshire form...

"I don't know what you're talking about..."

...reminded of the day he escorted the woman he eventually married, almost able to pull off this surprise.

They walk behind the two boys.

"I could have sworn Aegan hated me," Lamar begins.

"That's my best friend! Aegan don't hate anyone. Too lost in his own world, competing with himself; too good at everything... so focused. He gets that from mom. Even if I could compete, I don't want to. He always in everyone's mouth at school. The girls fawn over him... the guys want to be like him... ugh!"

Morocco marvels at the school's interior on his tour.

"Well, for what it's worth... I could only see you. Every. Time. You are what does it for me."

Lamar grabs Morocco's hand.

"Consent?"

"Implied!"

Lamar cradles their arms, clasping his free hand over the top in between pointing at the different rooms and features of the school.

They talk about that first night they met.

"Of course he told me, that's why I ran you down that day," Morocco confesses.

"Somehow, I knew you were coming to see me. Why did you just stand there?"

"I thought you were trying to date that girl, and I had misjudged if you like guys."

"Yeah... I figured as much. But I am out. I couldn't live my life hiding me, nor how I feel about you."

Denae wipes a tear, watching the pair in front of them.

"You are such a softie..." Marcus squeezes his wife.

"And you are such a clown," Denae refreshes her tissue.

"They strict?" Lamar wonders.

"They have actually been very accommodating this entire time. I am still trying to figure out some things as well. Aegan is a buffer for a lot: our younger brothers default to him, kids at school... well, we already went through all of that. He's likely going to U-town, if not a school here in Chicago, so he is always going to be around. I kind of feel bad pushing him away some, but he doesn't have to smother me, either."

Lamar is an only child, so he doesn't understand the dynamic Morocco describes.

"Sometimes, I wish I had a brother," Lamar laments.

"Borrow one of mine," Morocco offers.

"When do I get to meet them?"

Morocco turns coy, silently smiling.

The family prepares for the ride to University Park, Indiana for the national rugby all-star game at "Dear, Old U." Marlons and Washingtons traveling for one last chance to see Aegan play before wherever his next step is... highly expected to be in U-town.

"I'm driving down with my teammates, Roc... no, you cannot ride with me. Besides, you're bringing Lamar along, so there's not going to be room... and you're not going to be focused on me at all... and I need to be tuned in for this game today."

"But Lamar wants to get to know you a little better, too."

"He just wants to post something online... and I haven't told anyone where I'm going yet."

Aegan lies to his brother... looking away. A tell-tale sign.

"So... you told someone that's not me? That's not how this works." Morocco smiles.

Aegan puts his bag in his car and drives off. Morocco remains oblivious to his brother's cues. Aegan's not going to force his brother to choose him, that's not something Aegan has ever... or will ever... ask anyone to do. Besides, for the past few months, Morocco has made it clear that Aegan needs to step back and give him freedom.

"You can ride down with us."

Hannon and Joey invite the new young couple along. Lamar leans over to whisper to Morocco.

"How long have they been dating?"

"They're not a couple. Hannon's straight.

They're just best friends. Joey been coming around for years... need a DNA test or something cause he practically family."

"Yeah? Well, you still the cute one."

Lamar nudges Morocco with his nose. Morocco grabs his arm...

"Come see the house–"

"Don't be too long; we about to leave!"

Hannon and Joey joke around with the rest of the family.

"He ain't told nobody what his decision is?"; "He ain't leaving this area any time soon!"; "I thought he was just going to go to U-town, he loves the Bison!"

They all coordinate who's riding with whom and associated logistics for the afternoon, including bringing down the food... cause neither grandmother is missing the game to be stuck in some kitchen.

Mr. Marlon tires of the stairs, and is getting impatient. He's forgotten a lot about what he should remember.

"Marcus... you not playing with Eigan today?"
He ponders.

A new concern enters Denae's mind.

The inside of the house is relatively quiet. Lamar and Morocco head up to tour those rooms first.

"This is Hannon's room, but I am getting ready to make it mine since he's got his own place now."

"Dang, all these medals and stuff! Is that the trophy from the natty?"

Morocco rolls his eyes...

"Stop fawning over straightness."

Lamar cowers a bit...

"Aegan stays downstairs with y'all?"

Morocco rolls his eyes again...

"No... Mr. Wannabe has his own room. After Apollo and Artemis were big enough, he moved up here. No one is allowed in this room... Hannon was never really like that. Aegan always lets me follow him around anyway, so I get to sleep up here a lot with him. We always talk about everything."

"Everything?..."

Lamar wonder just how much these two share.

"EVERY thing!"

"So... you gon' tell him that I–"

Lamar reaches around the waist of his...

"Hey... what are we?"

He asks... as Morocco prepares to open the door to Aegan's room...

"IN TROUBLE... the hell y'all doing up there?"

Denae reenters to pack a few snacks for the young ones.

"I'm just showing him the house!"

"Morocco... if you don't get yo ass–"

The boys rush downstairs.

"Mmm hmm... your favorite, huh?"

Marcus smiles.

"Don't start with me, Marcus. Last thing I need is to hear Aegan's mouth on HIS day!"

Denae is already flustered... unsure of what Aegan is going to choose today.

She begins thinking about his namesake again. Marcus tries thinking for her.

"Eigan would be so proud."

"Of which one... Morocco is so open and free, and that's Aegan's doing. It's almost like he was always here looking over us. You know he's not going to Dear, Old, U."

"The hell you say... boy been repping the Bison since day one. He loves U-town!"

Marcus beams, and begins chanting:

"B... I... S,O,N: other teams will guess again!"

"Everyone is not a carbon copy of you, Marcus. He is you in so many ways, but you weren't as sure of yourself at his age."

"Aww, woman... what do you know–"

"I know my son. I just hope he stays close."

"U-town IS close." Marcus dismisses his wife.

Kissing and fondling Lamar just inside the door, Morocco hears his parents talking about his best friend... and gets a little worried.

He calls his phone...

No answer.

He shoos Lamar away... to text Aegan...

I can't wait to see you play for the Bison!

Three dots... and nothing.

Not that he would have told Morocco even if that was his decision, but Aegan would rather be silent... than lie. It hurts him to lie.

* * * * *

Driving down to U-town, Morocco is not nearly as handsy as he was earlier today. Lamar, thinking it has everything to do with being yelled at to 'stay in your seatbelts,' participates in the conversation coming from the front seat.

"Ugh... I haven't been home in a while," Joey rolls his eyes.

"Were you open in school?" Lamar interrupts.

"Joey ain't never been shy... why you ask?" Hannon answers.

"I'm still working through some things, like... everyone still reads me as straight: I hate that!" Lamar comments.

"Reads you as straight? Or as a guy? Cause those are two different things." Joey corrects.

Lamar ponders.

"Well... Morocco is a little more–"

"Watch it!"

Morocco chimes in... silencing Lamar.

"Morocco is himself... he was himself before you met him, and will always be himself. That's not going to change. He grew up in a loving and accepting house that didn't impose on him any preconceived notions of what he should do and who he should be. Heck... I venture to say that straight people have more trouble with authenticity because all of them are caricatures of what they think a man is." Joey responds.

"Tell me about Eigan."

Morocco wants to probe for clues about his brothers.

Joey looks out the window... Hannon struggles to respond.

"Eigan... was more special than you would ever understand. He's why dad doesn't beat your ass... if we're just honest. You know I would never be allowed to have a girl in the house... but I think, for him, he's afraid of you getting too many No's in life. So he tries to minimize your No's in the house... Aegan has always kept your No's away from you outside the house. That boy there!" Hannon laughs.

"Fuck you mean?"

"Aegan beats up bullies, man. He's always been that way. And when you came along, y'all were always close because I was the darling, especially on dad's side, as the oldest Washington grandchild. So Aegan finally had someone to look over and impress. I remember when he came to me and told me you were... different. He's so perceptive... we were still kids ourselves. I don't even think you knew you were gay. Anyone say something slick about you... he'd fuck 'em up. He was tiny back then, too... still would fuck up any and every one if he saw them picking on someone. I definitely wasn't like that."

Lamar looks at Morocco... who obviously never knew a lot about his brother.

"Hanjoon used to be in a group that went around protecting other gays... a few of them were at the funeral... called themselves the Salmon Squad. They were a bit violent in defending our community, they still feel a little guilty that they couldn't prevent what happened to one of their own..."

Joey continues looking out the window while thinking back to the service.

Reaching for a little lightheartedness in the weight of the moment...

"No one would ever call Joey effeminate... no one would ever say that about Hanjoon or Eigan, either. But they are all absolutely g-g-g-g... GAAAAAYYYYYYYY!" Hannon hollers...

Joey punches him.

"Oww man, that shit still hurts. I thought you didn't box anymore?"

"I'm your brothers' coach, dumbass!"

"Aegan sounds like Hanjoon... but I thought Aegan was named for Eigan?"

Morocco gets a little curious about his brother.

"He is... but what that got to do with anything? Hanjoon and Aegan play the same position on the pitch, both are unnecessarily smart... Aegan is kind of the best of Eigan and Hanjoon. All three of us spent a lot of time around those two, don't you remember?" Hannon beams.

"Dang, I never picked up on it... Aegan really is a little Hanjoon, huh?" Joey laughs...

then he pauses, looking out the window again.

"I miss my dads... I miss them so much."

"They left a legacy you can be proud of... and look, you even built your own without trying to outdo them or ignore what they accomplished."

Lamar looks at Morocco... who begins to cry a little. He now understands why Aegan feels differently about his decision to go to Sable... but he's not going to change his mind.

"I don't want to talk about this anymore."

Morocco opens his phone...

Aegan still has not responded.

*   *   *   *   *

"*What a performance...*"

Sports Reporters crowd the Parker home in U-town for one of the biggest announcements of the recruiting season.

Morocco stares at his brother... standing behind a table... mom and dad beaming in the background. He kisses his mom... and hugs his dad. Three hats in front of him: "Dear, Old U" in U-town; the flagship in Berkeley; the Institute in Atlanta. He looks so handsome in his uniform... repping the Academy in the vertical-stripe blues.

"This is all just a formality... your parents went to U-town... one of your mentors went to U-town... your brother went to U-town... every year... you go to U-town... so no one is going to be shocked... relatively speaking. U-town fans are buzzing online, impressed by what you did on the pitch today among some of the best in the nation! You're going to contribute to a program that's waiting on your arrival to help them get back to those glory days!"

"Of course I love U-town, that's never going to change. I owe a lot to this place... Dear, Old U will win a natty someday... just not against us..." Aegan reaches down and puts on a cap...

"I'm headed to Berkeley."

Aegan proudly confesses... staring at Morocco. The smile on his face... makes him look almost like his dad's twin... a Cheshire cat. Hannon hugs his brother... Denae and Marcus, though he is shocked, join in the family spectacle.

"Wow... I think that's going to upset a lot of people..." the announcer continues his segment on the live feed...

Morocco turns and walks off... followed by Lamar.

"He's so fucking selfish!"

The cameras file out... there's not much of a story here for the local outlets to cover. Aegan goes downstairs to change. Morocco follows him.

"You've always been such a selfish prick!"

Aegan washes his face and hands.

"Always have to do your own thing... no one else can shine because it's all about you! You can't even stay and endure one moment of someone else shining other than you!?"

Aegan walks around his brother, putting his sweaty Academy uniform in his bag, for the rugby jersey of his destination. A surprise gift from Mother Washington, who packed his gear just for old times' sake... including the snacks Hanjoon would leave him.

"You're supposed to always be here. Why are you so mad? Did you think being gay meant I wasn't going to find a partner? Are you jealous or something cause you bring no one home?"

He pushes buttons, but the machine is unplugged.

Instead of reacting, Aegan checks himself in the mirror... turns to face his brother... sidesteps him... and goes back upstairs to join the cookout. Morocco... stunned... as Lamar comes to find him.

"What's wrong?" Lamar asks.

Morocco forgets about consent and tackles Lamar...

"Holy shit..." Lamar exclaims, as they land on top of Aegan's bag.

Not intentionally... but conveniently.

"I've never done this before–" surprised at his boyfriend's actions.

Morocco is furious.

"But... here–? Holy fuck... that feels... oh no... stop!"

Lamar's body responds in opposition to his thoughts.

"Ugh... that's disgusting!"

Morocco doesn't like the taste... and spits it out...

All over his brother's gear.

Lamar slightly panics...

"Whose bag is that?"

"Who cares... fags are allowed to have sex!"

Morocco fixes Lamar's clothes and helps him stand up.

"You think your brother hates you for being gay? That sounds different from what we just heard on the ride down here."

"Hannon don't know shit... fuck him and fuck Joey, too."

Morocco heads upstairs.

Lamar... wavering between hiding what just happened, but not pissing off Morocco... follows.

Aegan ignores his brother, coincidentally; not intentionally, who is more visible with his boyfriend. Marcus and Joey's father, Dr. Adam Parker, talk about a few things that come with raising a gay kid. Aegan and Hannon are shouting down one of their conservative uncles... now being critical of Morocco's display with Lamar.

Aegan throws a punch... and proceeds to beat Uncle Arlen. The first swing was more than enough, but was not the end of the flurry. Hannon, unable to pull his brother off... why he even tried?

"AEGAN– IVEY– WASHINGTON!" stops him... as only a mother's voice can.

He throws arms off of him... stares down Morocco, who only glimpses a taste of his brother's might... and cowers a bit.

Marcus sips a beer.

"I told you not to piss him off today, Arlen. Press charges if you want to..."

as Serena begins to scold Marcus for not controlling his son... at the expense of her husband.

"I objected at the wedding... remember? I'm allowed to not hold my peace."

Marcus' standard reply when his sister tries to chastise him.

Denae pulls Aegan to the side.

"You can't be mad at Morocco for not wanting you to defend him anymore."

"It's not that, ma... that boy doesn't know what defense looks like... all he knows is being a contrarian. Sorry... that's not the type of gay man I am accustomed to."

Aegan goes downstairs to grab his bag...

"What the FUCK!?"

He runs back upstairs, no shirt on... his bag unzipped, and brand new jersey haphazardly laying on top.

"What now?!" Denae asks... to no response...

Aegan hops in his car... and drives off.

Uncle Mario, the oldest Marlon child, walks over to Morocco.

"You proud of yourself?"

Morocco turns his head away in defiance...

"Very."

Mario dials in.

"You're not the first gay child to be born in this family... and you won't be the last. You don't know how good you have it. We all gon' have your back, but whatever you just did to Aegan was never necessary... I don't care how you excuse it or justi-lie it."

"You're too old to understand anything," Morocco dismisses.

"What we not gon' do today... is disrespect me. I'm not your fucking mom, and she won't stop me regardless. There's a reason we're all here today... and whether or not you like it... Aegan deserves one day... and today was his day. You have that boy's attention 3 hundred and sixty five days of the year... every year... and you couldn't give him his one thing? He didn't do what he did to outshine you... he did what he did so you would always have something to be better than. He wasn't hurt when you rejected rugby for baseball. He was your biggest cheerleader. Found your dad's old stuff and helped you... while still keeping up with his own routine. He has strong examples of gay men living unashamed, and that influences how he treats you. Eigan... Hanjoon... me... Joey... he wants to be sure that you become your version of us... and not some statistic." Mario straightens the record.

"I didn't know you were gay..."

"You're the only one. I don't come around because of my own shit... but it's never because THIS family has ever made being gay an issue... save bruised boy over there," Mario points to Arlen. "Aegan gave you an example of a man... why do you hate that?"

"I don't hate that... it's just not the man I want to be."

"Well... you don't have to punish people who aren't the type of man you want to be, either. That's what society does to gay men everywhere... punishes us for not being their definition of man. Aegan has NEVER done that to you."

Morocco storms inside the house... Lamar stays behind to talk with Mario.

"Chil'... he battling wars that don't exist just to prove he has weapons," Mario dismisses Morocco.

Inside, Morocco sees Joey talking with some white guy, and realizes that no one cares. No one is monitoring the situation... or whispering behind his back about him being gay.

The kids at school are different from his family, that's for sure... but he projected their treatment on to his family... for whatever reason. And when he finally ran into Lamar...

'Why am I with Lamar? Just to prove that I am gay? Do I even like him, or am I using him to portray an image on to everyone? To prove how normal I am... or how gay I am... or maybe I just want a reaction from them?'

He's so confused.

He opens his phone to call Aegan... the call rings twice... then disconnects. He sends him a text.

No response.

He hasn't responded to the earlier messages either.

Morocco shrugs it off... and heads back outside.

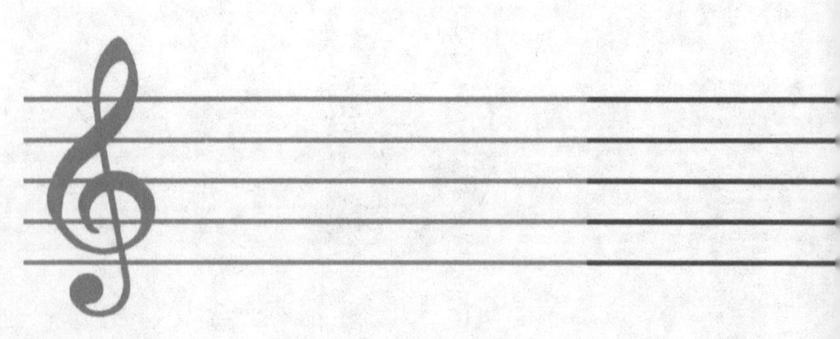

What a breath of fresh air being at Sable has been for Morocco. Summer tryouts... and he is sitting principal chair on horn. Aegan was principal trumpet at Academy... and their music program isn't nearly as respected as it is here. Morocco has already been tapped as a lead in a piece written and choreographed by a Sable graduate from a few years back who is working on Broadway. Aegan never had a piece written for him... and though he can dance... is nowhere near as agile and graceful as Morocco.

In addition to laying the foundation for his own legacy, seeing more gay guys in school opened him up in a way that he could only imagine straight kids enjoyed at Academy. They get picked on for being gay... here, you get picked on for not knowing who's in the finale for the drag competition.

That's normal things to get picked on for... right?

Lamar brought his boyfriend to every social event possible. Featuring him at the junior showcase; junior picnic; numerous upper-class parties and gatherings... and that was before the school year started.

As he walks down the halls of Sable... "that's Lamar's boyfriend"... being a stranger who is the center of gossip. He pretends to ignore the jealousy.

Lamar decided to play basketball again this season... 'who cares about being teased?'

"At least I got someone on my dick... all these girls around here and you can't get none?"

The teammates laugh along with Lamar... for once, a straight guy feels ostracized for HIS sexuality.

"Yeah... well at least I don't have to worry about shit dick. Who wants that? Or... are you doing the bending... for that!?"

James starts prancing around the gym with limp wrists.

Coach blows the whistle.

"I've told y'all about the gay jokes... Lamar... that's not an excuse to return hateful statements. Our policies don't change just because you're out the closet."

The players snicker...

"Gon' be brown in two or three places–"

One of them "thought" he whispered. Lamar lunges at Jackson.

"I'm still a fucking man, you bitch-ass nigga!"

"No means no, homo!"

The two boys swing at each other, but the teammates tackle Lamar... allowing him to receive a free kick to his face.

Coach tackles Jackson.

"Assault! You can't put your hands on kids!"

A few of the other players waver between participating and breaking up the melee.

* * * * *

Marcus and Denae catch the local news, learning about the suspension of The Academy's season. According to the investigation, students felt pressured to be in compromising situations around a gay teammate, obviously no student names were released to the public. The coach has been fired for 'not fostering a safe place for all players, regardless of sexual orientation;' and 'endangering the safety of students engaged in educational enhancement during post-school activities.'

"Championships don't matter to us... producing quality men and women does. And we cannot have teachers like this threatening our students... or putting an agenda on them..."

A few conservative parents praise the outcome.

"I don't remember seeing any of them at PT meetings," Denae chimes in.

Lamar refuses to talk to Morocco right now... and Morocco is not sure why.

"He won't tell me what happened, but I know he feels upset since there's no season. If only Sable had its own team..."

"Probably not enough guys at your school trying out for that to be a thing," Marcus considers.

"How do they have enough for a baseball team, but not a basketball team?" Morocco asks.

"Different skill sets. You go to a school that relies on people mastering difficulties. You have quick eyes and quick reflexes... and, you're my son. Not that basketball isn't difficult, but the barrier to entry is kind of low. Doesn't cost as much. Not that the people who attend Academy are poor, but folks at Sable got money. Y'all have a hockey team; ice skating is also a competitive sport for y'all. Academy doesn't have either." Marcus grins.

"Coach wants me to play..."

"Go for it!" Denae encourages.

"But I'm not trying to make the news... Lamar had a bruise on his head!" Morocco reminds them.

Marcus changes the channel.

"Since when are you afraid of fighting someone? Or getting in a fight?"

Since he no longer has his safety net.

For the first time in months... he reconsiders a few things. He looks up the season results out of Berkeley on his phone...

"They only lost one game this year."

Denae looks at Marcus, who continues changing channels... unphased.

* * * * *

Morocco sits in his room, anticipating a call from Lamar... he says he is ready to talk about a few things. Hannon's stuff is packed away, so this room is all his... right next to Aegan's room. He dare not go in there... he's seen it enough. Instead, he goes into his new closet... to find a fabulous winter outfit for "the runway" in the morning, last day of school before break. He takes a picture and sends it to Lamar.

Damn... that's a lot.

WYM

Lamar calls.

"You don't think you can tone it down just a bit?"

"No... why would I do that?"

"You weren't like this last year. Like bring that back some. I like DUDES."

"These are men's clothes... what the fuck?"

"Man... whatever... I'm not walking next to you if you wear that."

"We go to a school with a significant gay

population... this isn't even the most flamboyant post-lunch outfit of the semester... let alone morning appearance."

"I love you, but you're too much, sometimes."

"If I give less... you'll love less... and I'm not about that life."

"It just... I don't want people to think less of me because they don't know who the top and who the bottom."

"WHAT?! We haven't even done that yet and you're worried about crap—"

"Exactly... that's not natural, man."

"Lamar..." Morocco chooses a little understanding... "Is that what they said to you at practice that day?"

"Maybe..." Lamar pouts.

"Baby... tell me what they said."

Lamar recounts some of what happened at practice on that fateful afternoon.

"I guess I'm still struggling with some things, but I am not struggling with being in love with you."

"And that's all that should matter. Fuck 'em... why they worried about what you do with your dick anyway? Only one man has a right to that knowledge... and that's me!"

"You silly... my dick is my business alone."

"Let me find out you fooling with someone else... and you gon' learn some more about me," Morocco gets angry on the phone.

"You don't run me," Lamar smiles...

Morocco hears it through the phone.

"Smile now, cry later."

* * * * *

Marcus drops Morocco off at school the next morning... usual spot. Not the only one who understood the assignment, as last day recitals and performances are scheduled throughout the day. So, it's almost like going to the theatre on opening night.

"You're coming back at noon, right?"

Morocco has a special performance his parents bet' not miss.

"We will be here at eleven," Marcus drives off.

Entering the front door, getting ready for the first scheduled performance, which Lamar was supposed to sit next to him for... but...

Not only did Lamar enter with his letterman jacket on... he's sitting with the jocks... pretending he can't tell how gorgeous his man looks today. Morocco can see the confusion on Lamar's face: torn between what he is doing, and what he should have done.

It's a very emotive performance, especially for the first session. Morocco pretends the dancer on stage is what pulls tears from his eyes.

"You're toned down today," Jesse comments to Lamar.

"Eh... well," Lamar ignores it.

All of his performances were yesterday anyway, so it's not that surprising...

"But we always do it up big for last day of the semester..."

Jesse changes out of his costume into his outfit for the day.

"Yeah, well... not this year... damn, I'm not gay like that!"

Lamar yells at Jesse... then walks off... finding other athletes to hang around.

"So I guess now that there's no basketball season, you're good enough for us?"

The jocks kid Lamar. For whatever reason, this makes him feel normal.

Morocco's correct: they haven't even "done that"... and he's already being criticized for it.

He didn't even tell him some of the worst comments they made while holding him down. He didn't even tell him what they tried to do to him while coach was tackling Jackson.

He still feels like he can smell shit on his nose... he can still feel their fists trying to...

* * * * *

"Damn youngin's" crowd the adult patrons at Daddy Halsted's; but Morocco sits in a world by himself, only two slices left on his dish. Lamar never really wants to come because... you know... Boystown. But when Morocco wants to eat... he eats!

Recognizing him from school, one of the athletes walks over...

"How does the new kid at Sable know about

this spot?"

Morocco stays silent.

"Hi..."

The student leans over to Morocco.

"Oh... I don't talk to strangers"

Morocco dismisses, focused on his book: the latest gay erotica.

"I'm not a stranger, I'm Roman DuBois," he smiles, as if Morocco should already know.

"Learning your name does not mean you're not a stranger," Morocco turns a page.

"And yet... I've gotten two sentences out of you already."

Roman laughs and heads to the register. Morocco looks up. 'I know this bitch ain't–' as he wavers between reaction and exit.

"To go, Roman?"

The cashier, a fellow Sabelian, rings up his usual order.

"Nah, I'm going to stay."

"But don't y'all have–"

Roman waves the cashier out of his business... walking back to Morocco staring at him with attitude and a cocked head.

"Yeah, I'm like that. Pay me little mind. I'm not going to let you isolate, though... you sit alone a lot during the day."

"So you be checking me out or something?"

"Would that be wrong to do? Are men not allowed to be intrigued by Morocco?"

He turns, wrenching his face... 'the audacity!'

"We live in the age of consent, you should know better."

Morocco returns to his book.

"That's not a no... are men allowed to be intrigued by Morocco?"

Morocco scans his page, and the cashier brings Roman his food.

"Thank you."

Roman quietly eats... as the slices on Morocco's table get colder. He keeps hearing Roman's phone beep with calls and notifications... and then he realizes he's been on the same page for quite a few minutes.

"Do you consider yourself a man?" Morocco offers.

"Do *YOU* consider me a man?"

Roman wipes his mouth.

Morocco continues reading the same line over and over. Roman stands to leave...

"It doesn't get good until chapter nine."

Morocco looks up into his eyes...

Marcus sharpens his knives. Mother Marlon has prepared a spread worthy of kings for this Christmas, visiting with her daughter's family for this holiday. Denae's brothers are with their respective other sides of the family for this year; or, in the case of Mario, just didn't feel like being around the cold of Chicago. It's the second time this year that Denae's parents are in the windy city... her dad being a little more grumpy than usual.

"When you getting that business started?" He growls at Hannon.

"I still have one more year, gram-pa. Been working on a lot of coding and building a few things with some of the boys. We're diving into the tech space," Hannon informs him.

Mr. Marlon forgets he asked the question. He rubs his leg.

"When's the food ready, Anna?"

Travel is becoming more and more difficult.

"Why didn't you want to get it amputated?"

Denae asks for the nth time, seeing if he remembers why he kept it. Mr. Marlon scrunches his brow.

"Don't bother me," Mr. Marlon growls again.

Anna-Euis brings him a slice of sweet potato pie... which tames him for the moment.

"Where's Eigan?"

It's a new, but repeated question...

"Now, dad, you know Eigan has passed."

Denae continues setting the table.

He mushes the food in his mouth, reminding himself of the facts. 'Denae's friend or his grandson?'

"I thought he was in Berkeley?"

True for both, in a way... just at different times.

Morocco gets up and leaves, heading into the study until he hears the call for dinner. He doesn't care that it's his turn to carve the bird this year. He waits for Lamar... who hasn't consistently been available since they argued about the last day of the semester. He's going to be here in a few minutes anyway.

He opens his phone... still no reply from Aegan. He's been looking less and less... this habit dies a slow death.

The doorbell rings... he hurries to greet the people waiting outside...

"Merry Christmas, baby!"

Lamar is dressed in something a little more androgynous than he might typically wear... picked out for him by Morocco while they were Christmas shopping.

"Oh, my!"

Morocco loves what he sees... but was kind of hoping someone else would be on the other side of the door, as his thoughts return to unread messages.

They both head upstairs...

"Lamar is here... can we get started, dad?"

"Just a moment... where's your manners? Introduce him and his mother to the family."

* * * * *

Denae's parents retire to the main bedroom suite for the evening... her and Marcus, relegated to Hannon's old room, Morocco's current room. So, back to the communal residency with his brothers in the basement. All of them want to play with Lamar. They were too young to meet any of the girls Hannon brought around; and Aegan never brought anyone around... so this is a new experience for them.

"Ya'll be kissing and stuff?" Jermaine asks... the twins giggle.

Lamar restrains himself a little bit, since the kids are too young to understand a lot.

"I don't kiss my boyfriends," Jermaine chastises. "I kiss the girls," he giggles.

"You don't have boyfriends... you have friends who are boys. That's different," Morocco corrects his brother.

"How is that different?"

"Because it is," Hyun silences Jermaine.

Hyun is in middle school right now, so he's already seeing some couplings. Might even have a girlfriend himself... being a dreamboat kind of runs in the family.

"Getting all these cards and gifts from your classmates," Morocco laughs.

"That's cause they know who my brothers are," he beams. "I can't wait to go to Academy, man. Put 'em boff to shame."

He mimicks passing a rugby ball.

Morocco, not sure how to respond to feeling looked over in more ways than one... gives a simple... "Go get 'em, Tiger."

Hyun goes off to play his video games, drawing Jermaine's attention as well. Bassel comes over...

"Is gymnastics similar to dance?"

Bassel tries to console Morocco, who stands up.

"I need to see Lamar out..." as he takes him to the front door.

"You ok?"

Lamar, being guided by the hand.

"You see me in a way no one else sees me; I love you."

"You don't mind that I am still working through some stuff?"

"You're working through it... not wallowing in it."

"Oooo, baby."

Lamar leans in to kiss Morocco, who pulls him in to his face. Lamar rubs his hands down Morocco's back, as he feels the hands of his boyfriend running through his hair... caressing his neck.

Morocco backs them into the library... closing the door, locking it.

"I wasn't planning–"

"Shhhhh... it doesn't always have to be planned."

Morocco takes off his clothes... and Lamar follows his example.

They both stare at each other's bodies... not sure what to do next.

"Well, it doesn't look like we will need lube," Morocco observes.

"Is it going to leave a spot?"

"I don't know... I don't care."

He lays on his back... and Lamar...

* * * * *

Sunlight catches the two boys asleep; fortunately, before most of the house has a chance to wake up. The mystique of jolly elves has been broken by older brothers long ago, so no one really gets up early in the house on Christmas Day... fortunate for Lamar to make an escape, especially since the study is by the foyer.

The alarm on the front door wakes Marcus and Denae out of their sleep.

"I'll kill him!"

Denae puts on her robe to head downstairs.

"At least he did it here," Marcus reasons.

"You're surprisingly ok with this. If Hannon would have done that here, you would have lost it!"

"Yeah, but Hannon isn't gay. I don't know; I feel like Morocco is testing us. He wants a reason to call us homophobes... in spite of all evidence. I am not trying to give in to his intentional disruptions."

Marcus quiets the alarm from his phone.

Denae thinks about it. It's not like any children will be born if they did 'do what they better not be doing in my house.' But where to draw the line? It's not obvious to many, but Lamar is a distraction from Aegan. They are completely different. Not that Morocco's feelings aren't genuine, but he is a lot more demonstrative in response to the freedom he enjoys in Aegan's absence.

*   *   *   *   *

Morocco still wants an answer to a question he asked over holiday break. Lamar contemplates a new experience... baby steps. He's already changing a lot about himself; but never really thought about crossing this additional line.

First day of spring semester... a special performance from the local ballet company to welcome the students for the last half of the year. The fashion show commences the daily activities. Morocco has to make an entrance... and this time... waiting for him at the front doors... dressed to impress...

"Let's go get 'em," Lamar takes his hand.

He escorts Morocco to first session, and then he and Jesse head off to independent study.

Whispering in the library...

"Morocco wants to... um... do to me what I did to him..."

Lamar has trouble with the thought. He's still a little traumatized from the incident that got the basketball team suspended.

Jesse, not really trying to think about the sexual habits of his friend, bemoans being a needed ear.

"What's the dilemma?"

"I've never... you know... bottomed before. He and I don't really have that dynamic: oral until it goes there... then I'm always on top."

Lamar embellishes, which he hopes doesn't disrespect Morocco, but certainly not at the expense of uplifting himself.

"I didn't even know y'all were fucking... but, there's nothing wrong with that," Jesse dismisses.

"I know, so why does he want to change it up?"

Lamar wavers, because he does find Morocco attractive.

"I think some guys view it as a dominance thing. It's not that they don't want to bottom: they don't want to feel effeminized. And being on top or bottom has nothing to do with any of that... that's heterosexual foolishness. He wants to experience all of you... don't you want to experience all of him? Even if it is just one time?"

Lamar rolls his eyes.

"I don't know, man... I guess that makes sense. But ain't no man going to dominate me, period! Fuck that noise you talking. Has nothing to do with sex, my guy."

"I mean... you want to end your relationship because your partner wants to have sex with you... What kind of foolishness is that?"

"Nah, I don't think I'm going to break up with

him... just want him to stop asking."

Lamar is not trying to go there. He still has to deal with fellow athletes who are less than welcoming to anything gay.

'How can you take it?'
'Do you ever get clean once you're done?'
'Can't trust nothing you say one you put your lips back there!'

Lamar knows he likes men, but he is not ready to give up every thing just yet. Besides, he doesn't really view Morocco like that.

"So which is it... you don't want to feel like less of a man... or you think I am already less of a man, and it will make you less-er of a man?"

Morocco isn't tired of this discussion just yet, but Lamar has had enough. It's no longer up for debate. Since Morocco won't submit...

"It's over. Leave me the fuck alone!"

Lamar disconnects the call.

Morocco, in his bedroom: blindsided. Feeling more alone than ever before. He considers going into the room next to his, but no sense in giving THAT power. Morocco pushed Aegan so far away, that now he is in California... not wanting to talk to any of his family, relatively speaking. Maybe he should just be happy and let Lamar figure it out on his own. Well... now that they have broken up... Lamar will absolutely have to do it on his own.

"I didn't think it really mattered. Does he see me as some woman or something?"

Morocco never felt like anything other than an

absolute man. He needs to clear his thoughts, not sure if he wants to feel insulted, or 'is being treated like a woman an upgrade to being treated like a gay man?'

On his own journey, finding his own happiness... taking pride in his own strengths and assets... he knows he should call Aegan, but is adamant about figuring this out.

It's a long weekend... the holiday season was so special, 'why can't Lamar understand that I don't see him as anything other than who he is?'

News travels fast, 'damn social media whores,' as apparently Lamar has posted the breakup. School on Tuesday is a bit awkward, with classmates buzzing about it. Morocco is a lot more private than his wanna-be-superstar-boyfriend... EX-boyfriend. But, unlike people who shall not be mentioned... Lamar needs the popularity.

Morocco grabs his tray during lunch, walking past the table with the hockey players... annoyed that they congregate so close to the end of the line.

   "HaaaaAAAAY MOROCCO!" they say in unison and laugh.

Morocco rolls his eyes and goes to sit with a few of the social rejects on campus. Roman enters the dining hall. Morocco can't hear everything Roman says, but the hockey team surely can. He exits the dining hall, and the teammates dissipate. One of them wanders over to the table with Morocco.

   "Sorry about the guys, we didn't mean anything by it. It's just... there's a lot of guys here who want to get to know you. Don't restrict yourself to assholes."

He walks off.

Morocco blushes a little bit. He scarfs down his food, then heads to the gym to talk about late tryouts for baseball season. 'A lot of guys want to get to know me,' encourages him... since it's coming from an athlete.

Civics class covers "Voices in Politics," and Morocco wants to focus on gay politicians and the contradiction of gay conservatives.

"I suggest you watch this documentary from 2009. It's a pretty good start, even though a lot of those names are no longer relevant. No one has really done an updated version of it, and there's a few high profile people who might get covered if they were to do a remake. You know... there's that anti-gay senator who died from covid... Senator Maher. There are rumors about his life, but being solicited isn't the same as being outed. And that's about all they can confirm. No one knows why he and his wife got divorced, but there are a few anti-gay senators who did come out or were outed... as this documentary highlights. Mainly because they were careless..."

Mr. Wilson drones on, obviously excited and studied on this topic... which seems to be avoided by students at Sable, in spite of it being an accepting institution. He brought up the late senator... which reminds Morocco of something that happened a few years back.

The house is conveniently quiet. As Morocco enters,

Marcus is home earlier than usual. He's in the kitchen... washing a dish, now empty of something he probably shouldn't have eaten; but it was worth any argument his mom is going to give him on her temporary visit. Besides, they can order in tonight.

"Hey!?"

He says with a stuffed mouth, as if the food isn't clogging the exit for his greeting. He shovels some attempts to escape back between his lips.

"I got this documentary from the library, I'm going to watch it again tonight at home," Morocco leads.

"Oh... what's it about?"

Marcus wants to savor the morsels, not force them down because of this conversation.

"Closeted politicians with anti-gay agendas."

Morocco sets his bag down, deceptively haphazard, as he opens the DVD player... and places the disc inside.

Marcus pauses.

"Um hmm," still wanting to savor this delicacy.

"It's kind of old, but my teacher was saying something about how it could be updated with a few people. You remember when Hannon was in school?"

Morocco scrolls through the menu screen. Marcus grunts in agreement.

"You remember that day Senator Maher came over? You remember what I asked you?"

He pauses just before pressing "start" on the

screen.

"What are you trying to asking me now, Morocco?"

Marcus, annoyed now that he couldn't savor the food he snuck home to devour.

"I asked you if he knew Eigan the way Hanjoon knew Eigan," Morocco reminds his father.

"And my answer ain't changing... NO: he didn't!"

Marcus finishes washing the dish, placing it on the drying rack.

"So did they have a relationship or not?"

Morocco doesn't need to know, just... not sure why he needs to know.

Marcus mulls a few things over.

"That's not what you asked me before, why does it matter now?"

"I don't know, dad. I keep being told about legacies of people... I'd hate to think Uncle Eigan would have dated such an..."

Morocco pauses.

"Remember Eigan the way you want to remember Eigan. People are allowed to change... people are allowed to stay the same. People are also allowed to revert to their old ways. Sometimes... men like you to be who they want you to be. Sometimes, they like you for who you are. That's in politics, friendship, relationships. You decide if you give them access to you. Don't let love cloud your judgment; but you get to decide who accesses you, and how they access you. Is this about Lamar?"

"NO... this is about a school project!"

Morocco presses play on the remote.

"Just because your mom isn't here, doesn't mean you get to raise your voice at me, jit. I'm not one of your little fucking friends. Now... don't put any of that senator's business in your report. You don't have the right to reduce Eigan to someone else's shame and fear. I don't give a fuck about Chase... but you're not going to disrespect Eigan. I said what I said about Chase... and I did not lie."

Marcus leaves his son to his thoughts, heading upstairs to take a nap... toothpick in hand.

Lamar breathes a sigh of relief. Morocco has agreed to stop asking. He's very secure in who he is, and he does like his time with Lamar. Making the baseball team also boosts his confidence, which was fortunately short a few players. More concerned with the excitement of tomorrow, he doesn't put his best effort into studying for an important math test. Eh, stuff like that comes naturally to him anyway.

"Chil'... you want me to make all that for just two people?"

The new nanny does not revel in being a chef for the evening.

"Please?!?!?!"

Morocco wants the night to be memorable, especially since Marcus and Denae won't be in town. They're going to go visit 'the special one'... during an observance for Julian Jee, or at least that's what Hanjoon went by in college to feel more "American." Some big match-up... Morocco ignored most of the conversation surrounding that topic.

* * * * *

It's the annual student government fundraiser for Valentine's Day. Definitely all the class presidents are helping, so it's going to be a long day for some of them. Buckets of roses get delivered... all red as the order specifies. As they arrive... a single pink one has made it in the mix.

The senior class president hides it... his sister likes that color.

Though Lamar is a member of student government, he is not helping out this year. It got embarrassing first year when he was writing his own secret admirer cards the morning before handing them out to... himself; but he revels in receiving all the roses delivered to his classes throughout the day. He considered volunteering again this year, since everyone should know he is going steady-ish with Morocco... but he's going to stay away.

For Morocco... this will be a new experience. Academy stopped handing out roses as a fundraiser for environmental reasons, and because some of the boys were uncomfortable receiving roses with coded language from secret admirers. They didn't like getting teased for being an unknown gay boy's crush. Morocco already felt isolated as it is: the girls weren't sending him flowers because he is gay... and even though he would have proudly walked around with a rose, what guy would sign up to send him one without being subject to the bullying that Aegan always defended him from; not to mention that Aegan didn't even care about not receiving any flowers.

Morocco rolls his eyes thinking about his brother.

This year is going to be different. He is guaranteed to get something! Plus, it's just a fundraiser for school. Fifteen dollars isn't a lot... and he's spending much more than that for tonight's dinner and a few other gifts that don't need to be given at school.

First session, Lamar walks him to class... no surprise there. Deliveries don't start until next period anyway. He's not going to see him until the end of second period, so there's time for him to get it right.

Not a lot of people in first session received any

gifts... but "I'm not just anybody..." so... he's not going to trip just yet.

He passes by Lamar's locker... which has been covered with... crap! Not sure if he should tear it down or not... though he does receive 'I like what you did with your boyfriend's locker' congratulations from random people.

Second session is theatre... so it makes more sense for him to receive flowers in here anyway. Feeling a little forgotten, he ends up tweaking his ankle on a simple plié. He decides to just sit out the rest of the session... making comments to the other dancers as they prepare for the Spring Showcase. He's got baseball workouts this afternoon as well... so now this day feels much longer than when it started. He limps a little, waiting for the theatre aide to at least bring a wrap out the back...

then Lamar is too late to escort him and give him a peck.

'I didn't study anyway,' he decides to skip.

This is getting worse.

Lamar received a lot of flowers... again. He's not sure what to do with them, but carrying them around while having to explain himself to Morocco was not a part of the plan. He is too embarrassed to throw the flowers away or show Morocco how much he is admired... not knowing if Morocco would have received any. 'Everyone should know... this is disrespectful on so many levels.'

He takes his stash to his mom's office... wondering what he should do.

"Well, I don't think avoiding him is advisable.
Face it head on... if he gets mad, he gets mad.
You can't control either side of this... but you
can control how you respond to it."

Even though Lamar intentionally slows the pace of
their relationship, maybe this is still moving a bit too
fast for them. Or maybe people don't realize he is
serious about Morocco. He's considering options...
as girls walk though the buildings with teddy bears
and chocolates... guys walk around with their roses,
or other displays of affection.

He finds Jesse.

"Hey, man, I don't know what to do with all
this. Last thing I want to do is make Morocco
mad. It's going good between us right now.
Can you help me out?"

"Just throw them away!"

"No... I don't want to hurt anyone's feelings,
but I also want them to all understand I am
pretty serious about him."

Jesse thinks of suggestions and people who can
help. Lamar needs to expand his circle... plenty of
schoolmates would love this task.

"I have an idea... see if you can skip until after
lunch... what's his last class?"

Jesse begins to plot.

* * * * *

Morocco eats lunch alone. Lamar isn't answering
any messages, and hasn't been seen all day, at least
not by him.

'Ooo, why you bought all those flowers for Lamar?'; 'Oh, all them not from you?'; 'He has a lot of admirers, you need to step up your game'...

There's a lot more competition in things outside the classroom here. The bullying isn't in opposition of who he is... it is in "honor" of who he is.

How confusing!

That hockey player who's been making eyes at him all year, sees him sitting alone... and brings him a rose...

Roman is quietly fine. He's very unassuming; and though he lacks a lot of bravado, he is absolutely authoritative and dreamy... wearing his number 76.

"Now, you know I'm with Lamar."

"Every new guy gets a rose, we leave no one behind."

Roman leaves the flower next to him.

It's pink: a different color from what most people are receiving, so 'who is handing out pink roses to new students?' Morocco searches the dining hall.

Taking note of the absent gifts on Morocco, Roman wants to touch him; but respects the relationship...

"He's popular, it's probably nothing more than that going on right now. He's likely thinking about you... don't worry."

then walks off... taking his tray to eat with his teammates.

Morocco's math teacher comes to find him.

"This is abnormal, never would have pegged

you for someone who would miss a math anything."

Mr. King, on lunch monitoring duties.

"I hurt my ankle in theatre... I'll come during my open period to take it, if that's ok," Morocco suggests.

"I highly recommend you do."

He leans over...

"I know it's been a bit of a culture shock for you this year, but I know what stock you come from. Your history precedes you. Don't dim your own light simply because you're surrounded by other stars... MAURY, absolutely NOT!"

He walks off to handle a situation.

Morocco finishes his lunch, then heads to his open period, with a brief stop by math to get that off his back. And then some time to go over his monologue for oratory class.

* * * * *

It's the end of the day... Roman smiling at him gives him a little encouragement. All he can think about is how many times he rehearsed this with Lamar. He sets up his props, in his costume... ready to perform.

"-mirroring and magnifying each other's light..."

He's fine with it. He knows Lamar is coming over tonight anyway, so nothing changes between them. If anything, Roman gives him a little bit of clarity. He can't expect everyone to just part like the Red Sea, simply because he's in the picture. Until he gets the official word that this is over... again... he is going to trust the boy he loves.

"... we are that person for another."

Morocco finishes.

"Lovely... what inspired you to choose this work?"

Mrs. Taylor makes a few notes on her tablet.

"The author is a gay, Black man. Even though we have many people making a name for themselves, it's always good to give an homage to the legacy left by those who come before us..."

Roman taps his pencil on his desk, smiling at how smart Morocco is. Morocco fails to ignore it. As the period ends, Roman catches up to him at the front of the class.

"You always speak so beautifully, you trying out for any of the plays?"

Roman walks alongside Morocco as they head to the door of the classroom.

"I don't know yet, baseball season will take a lot out of me and I–"

They both turn...

Standing right outside the doorway, is Lamar... with about 2 dozen roses in an arrangement.

"You thought I forgot about you, didn't you?"
Morocco is a bit speechless.

"I'm going to be honest, these are all mine... but everything I have is for you. While everyone sees me... all I see is you... my clear-eyed person... my mirror," Lamar recites.

Morocco turns to Roman, who understands, and walks off... slightly defeated. Nothing discernible to Lamar, but Morocco and Roman know what just happened.

Lamar sits in the stands... boiled peanuts are his new thing... first convinced on the delicacy during the holiday season, one of Mr. Marlon's favorite snacks.

Lamar spits the shells to the side as he scans the nine players on the field... still trying to get the hang of it... staring at one in particular.

He sees that baseball cap with the "S" on it; and the shimmer of a thin chain around the neck of the boy at that position. Upside-down sunglasses on his head... just enough of the shirt opened up that he can see the attempts of chest hair on his body.

Lamar gets a little hot under the collar.

The guy at... position 5?... adjusts his pants... again... shaking out his cleats... a few bounces...

'All that cake!'

Those thighs... those calves...

  PING!

Lamar's face snatches to home plate, just as he hears the thud of ball hitting mitt... plucked out of the air by number 15... his former position in a previous sports endeavor.

"THIRD OUT... SABLE WINS!"

THE ANNOUNCER SHOUTS INTO THE PA SYSTEM.

  "Did you get that?" Dr. Barnes asks Lamar.

  "Yup... that's MY man!"

The baseball teams congratulate each other... and Morocco runs over to the fence.

  "Hey, baby!"

"Hey... you did so good out there!"

"You have no idea what you're looking at, do you?"

"Um... no... but I am learning. I see that third stop is such an important position."

"Emphasis on learning..."

Morocco kisses Lamar, then heads to the dugout. A few parents from the opposing school frown at the spectacle.

"I would feel that way even if I saw a player kissing their girlfriend..."

One of them has to proclaim loudly while walking by... as she 'doesn't see' one of the teammates actually kiss his girlfriend.

Morocco ignores it.

"Want to go to the center when I get done?"

"Can I just meet you there? Let me take my mom home."

Lamar holds back a little, the critique from strangers becoming more important.

"Boy, I been walking this city for decades... go be with your boyfriend."

Dr. Barnes heads off.

Lamar sits in his car... waiting for Morocco to get done with his team obligations. They have to clear the field and set it up for tomorrow's game... hoping to get a sweep in the series.

"Like... how do y'all do it?" Jason asks.

"We just do... like, I don't know what to say.

We like each other. All that other crap coming from homophobes doesn't mean anything to us."

"Yeah, I can't even fathom not bringing home the right girl. And here you are just slinging dudes and stuff."

"I'm not slinging dudes... just one dude. And I do have a supportive family, but they can't tell me nothing about who I'm dating."

"What do your brothers think about it?"

"What did I just say?"

"Damn, ok... you don't have to be so touchy."

"Let's just put the equipment up..."

Morocco is getting some attention for how well Sable is doing on the diamond; their record is pretty decent. He feels a little pressure because both his brothers drastically improved their teams... and he can't seem to do the same. He has to remind himself that he plays because he enjoys playing.

"Why does everyone think we just sleep around?" Morocco breaks his own request.

"I don't know... that's just what we've always been taught. Y'all inherently lack morals or something... like, aren't y'all born with HIV or something like that? Isn't that how they can tell?"

"Are you that ignorant?"

"I'm not trying to be, I'm asking... I thought you didn't want to talk about this!"

Morocco walks off, heading to the locker room.

Lamar opens his phone...

"Yeah, what's up, bay?"

"Um... can we go get tested?"

"Tested? For what? You don't trust me or something?"

"What's that got to do with anything? Should I not trust you?"

"What the hell! You showing signs or something? You gave me something?"

"That's absurd!"

"Then why you asking me that shit?"

"How do I know I'm your first?"

"You don't know that, you just have to trust that you are. Why would I lie about that?"

First boy, just so we're clear.

"I still want to go get tested... and if you are not ok with that... then that just proves you don't care about me."

"You're exhausting, you know that? We can go get the test... and then you can find another boyfriend!"

Lamar disconnects the call.

Morocco comes out... throws his bag in the trunk... and they drive to the center in silence.

Morocco is not interested in dating anyone. He breathes a sigh of relief that the whole Lamar fiasco is over. It is already a big deal in high school social dynamics when athletes date each other; add to that the sometimes unnecessary spectacle when gay men end relationships:

IGNORING AS YOU WALK PAST EACH OTHER... SNAPPING HEADS OF DISAPPROVAL... THE 'HE SAID/SHE...' ER UM, 'HE SAID/HE SAID' AS EACH IS "OVER IT," BUT JUST HAS TO TELL THEIR SIDE OF THE STORY. THE ATHLETES HAVE ALREADY DECIDED WHICH SIDE OF THE FORMER COUPLE THEY ARE GOING TO DEFEND. PEOPLE PICKING BASED ON WHO THEY KNOW... OR WHO THEY LIKE... AND SOME FOLKS WHO AREN'T INTERESTED IN THE DETAILS, BUT THEY ARE AWARE OF THE SITUATION.

Roman meets at a bistro bookstore on North Halsted.

"I was kind of shocked that you messaged me. I am not a rebound, Morocco."

More than aware of the breakup, but he also thinks about the way Morocco looked at him at Daddy Halsted's that afternoon. He missed an important school meeting just to be around Morocco, and exchange with his energy.

"Roman, stop, you and I have known each other for a little while now. We're not dating, just hanging out,' Morocco corrects, a slight blush.

"I'm just letting you know. I enjoy your energy. I like talking with you. I've seen your revues, you have a presence. You're so smart. How you get like this?"

Morocco can't really decide what emotion he is supposed to have, but something about this feels expectedly natural.

"I've been told that before..." he shies away.

"Yeah, but how often do you tell yourself, and more importantly... how often do you believe it?"

Morocco hates how Roman sees him... not visually, metaphysically. He sees his existence, not his attraction.

Roman is like a hidden asset at a garage sale, with everyone clamoring over other items they believe are more worthy... then you get your stash appraised, and someone tells you... 'do you realize what you have here?' He is coincidentally statuesque; confident; insanely gorgeous. Morocco likes Roman's glasses... they make him look competent, but when he jokes... they make him look goofy. It's the duality that makes Morocco curious.

"Why are you in a speech class? You don't even need that past second year."

"It's independent study. One of my sisters has an impediment, but I think I actually want to go into linguistics."

Roman likes to praise him in different languages. Morocco caught on quickly, and keeps the translate app open on his phone with the auto-detect setting activated. Roman just smiles when he sees Morocco try to hide a blush while discovering what he said.

"You have nothing but sisters, and I have nothing but brothers." Morocco laughs.

"Yeah, my sisters are older than I am and they all went to Sable. I can't get away with anything. But we don't have a women's hockey team... so I got them there. They used to beat me up all the time. But now... their boyfriends are scared of me... the sissy boy," Roman laughs.

"Ain't nothing sissy about you," Morocco nuzzles.

Roman feels the affection between two... people... who are "not dating."

"You neither..."

Roman caresses Morocco's face, holding his chin in his thumb and forefinger. There's a glisten in Roman's eyes that Morocco never really saw before... and he wants to—

"Are you sure?"

"Roman... I don't know what's going on, I just know... I... there's so many things I want to say to you. I just don't know how," Morocco turns away.

"I think I get it. If I'm honest, I can feel everything you want to say when you're with me. I can't explain it either."

A hint of uncertainty that comforts Morocco... who decides now may not be the right time to kiss this almost-man: legal age outweighing persona. Normally, when he has a crush, he would talk to—

Morocco pushes away.

"I'm sorry, I shouldn't have said anything. Just, I want to take it slow because I am sure about you, Morocco. This isn't a crush... it never was a crush. You supplement me."

"They're getting ready to lock up, we should go."

As they leave, he reaches behind him to grab Roman's hand. Denae would be proud... IYKYK.

* * * * *

It's so rare for a sophomore to get asked to senior events, especially at this time of year; but who is going to say no to Roman DuBois?

"No, we're not a couple, I just like being around him."

Roman protects Morocco's dignity while being berated with notions of 'Lamar's leftovers.' The two, navigating the remainder of their respective sport's seasons, find time to be around each other where possible after school. Unable to see each other play, they stay as invested as possible in each other's success. On the rare times they both have no games, Roman takes Morocco home after school, driving a beautiful luxury coupe. It's understated: all matte, emblem blends in with the car finish... signature Roman style.

Taking advantage of the freedom established when he was with Lamar, Morocco spends some evenings with the DuBois family, but nothing overnight: Roman sets that boundary. It's a lot quieter than being at home with all his brothers being boisterous on random evenings... and usually the evenings he needs peace and quiet.

The chef for the DuBois Family cooks a fine meal for

the evening; possibly coincidence. Roman makes his surprises subtle, so the dessert looked interestingly familiar: a deconstructed take on strawberry shortcake. Morocco smiles.

Dr. and Mother DuBois allow the boys to have their privacy...

    "but keep that door open!"

The two boys watch TV, with Roman's dog curled up in front of them.

    "Oooo, let's watch this movie?" Roman suggests, Morocco accepts.

* * * * *

Roman awakens in a bit of a panic, which slightly jolts Morocco. The movie credits are rolling. He kisses the head on his chest, "It's almost late."

Morocco looks up at Roman...

It may have been drowsiness, it may have been confusion...

The dog isn't in the room to witness what will become an intense, but quiet scene... as Roman is quickly overwhelmed by the first touch between them in all of their exposure.

Morocco will get home well after the late evening news. At least it's not a school night.

In spite of their breakup, Lamar still knows who he wants to marry someday... but Morocco appears to be pretty sold on Roman.

"What you giving that boy? Sable might actually make the playoffs on the diamond this year!"

One of Roman's teammates laughs.

"None of your business. Give less to yo' girl and maybe we can make the playoffs, too!"

Roman isn't happy that they are struggling on the ice for his last season... but he is proud that the baseball team is making a buzz across campus, and the city.

Denae and Marcus, in the stands for one of the last regular season games on the home diamond. Morocco doesn't feel like showering, just is ready to leave once the game is over... hoping to make senior day on the ice.

"Your favorite spot?" Marcus asks.

"Yes, Roman is going to take me for some 'za and 'da. I might get a sub tonight, too. I'm really hungry."

"Well, when do we get to meet this... Roman?! And that's not how you ask permission," Denae corrects.

"Ma, please?! I REALLY like him!" Morocco pleads, quietly.

"Then we're coming, too!"

Denae, ready to meet this boy taking all her son's time.

As the three enter Daddy Halsted's, they are shocked to find the popular restaurant coincidentally quiet; though there's another family inside. Morocco turns to his parents...

"I didn't know about all this, can we go, please?"

Morocco can't appreciate the universe's timing.

"Absolutely not," Denae proceeds.

Marcus follows his wife's lead. Morocco knows there's no refuge there, and his dad is going to enjoy watching Denae get the best of her "favorite child."

The father of the other family stands... Marcus greets him first, as Denae walks over to his wife.

"Hiram DuBois, huh? How come we have never met before?"

Marcus shakes his counterpart's hand.

"Our circles do not intertwine, apparently. You're northside, we're out of Bronzeville. Why didn't you move there? Or even to Austin?"

"We got a good deal on some land, probably should have done a little more research on neighborhoods here. But we also wanted to be close enough to Boystown that Eigan and Hanjoon could drop by anytime."

"Oh, ya'll knew them?" Hiram laments.

"Practically family... they'd still be integral parts of bringing up the boys. In fact, my two oldest kids are highly influenced by both of them."

"Oh, they gay too?"

A little shock comes across Hiram's face.

"I don't think so, but that's none of my business," Marcus corrects.

"True that," Hiram concedes.

Morocco wants to run from the display, but he knows Roman is on the way, and he really wants to see him. He's kind of mad at his parents for coming along, and mad that Roman's parents are here.

'This is our thing,' he pouts to himself, nodding to the cashier, who knows what Morocco usually orders... though he is not sure he has much of an appetite.

He thinks back to the day they met, while feeling a little crowded in the restaurant. A familiar hand touches his waist.

"You want to leave, don't you?"

Roman whispers in his ear... swooning Morocco. That sultry sound, that tickle on his ear... that breeze across his neck. Roman has no clue how his innocence just turned into arousal. Morocco reaches up to grab Roman's neck, surprising even him, but Roman caresses nonetheless.

"Um... that's my son!"

Marcus breaks the concentration.

"I know."

Roman gently lets go... as Denae pulls Marcus by her left hand.

"You must be Roman? We have heard too much about you."

Denae stretches out her right hand.

"Um... if it's ok... can I just wait here a bit? No

disrespect."

Roman was a little crouched to embrace Morocco, and if he fully stands... it's going to hurt.

Denae recoils a bit.

"Wow, you're honest to a fault."

She turns to Marcus...

"He's an honest one!"

Marcus' eyebrows raise. He gives an approving nod with a downward smile.

"You can ask him anything... and he won't lie to you."

Hiram beams with pride.

"We know..."

Denae, cautious about mentioning his name. Marcus leans down and informs Hiram...

"Morocco's best friend is just like that."

Julian and Aegan have been friends since the Washingtons lived in Cali. He was ready to enroll at 'Dear, Old U," but changed his mind when he found out before Aegan's announcement.

That's how close they are.

Growing up, they did not have the fortune of playing on the same rugby teams. Now, in college at Berkeley, their friendship has grown stronger since Aegan drove out west. Julian knows what Morocco did; and he welcomed Aegan into his home, with his parents' permission, of course.

Aegan prefers playing scrum-half, Julian prefers playing fly-half. They both believe they play each other's position better.

Mother Washington would have gladly bought him a house to stay in, but he wanted to live on campus. She moved out to Cali... 'a little sick of the cold weather.' Every Sunday, the rugby team shows up for dinner. She loves the company and attention. It started out with just Julian and Aegan, but then Ram joined in; followed by a few other nosey teammates... wondering why those two never ate with the team on Sunday.

On any random day, Julian and Aegan get back to their dorm room... proud of each other. Outside of school and practice, no one really knows what they do... just know they like to test limits. They are going to get in trouble if they keep staying out late; so on some occasions, like tonight, they make curfew.

   "So... she didn't know you bust?"

Julian listens to Aegan recounting the night he and that girl from the protest hooked up, as they prepare for bed.

"Man, if she did, she ain't say nothing," he laughs. "I just kept licking her nipple until I got hard again. It took a little longer... but I bust again: embarrassing! I just kept going since it didn't go down."

Aegan and Julian laugh.

Though Aegan is very accustomed to high intensity situations, sex is its own kind of drama. He wanted to explore her body, a bit of sensory overload... nothing that she would ever perceive. She came while his tongue probed... and his stroke game lacks nothing... She struggled to suppress her responses.

"You sure this is your first time?"

Add two more things he is good at.

"Oh... she was creamin' you? Dude. If she was shaking... I'on know, they can fake it, though. You going to see her again?"

"I'd like to... She said she wants to do a threesome, though."

Aegan prefers something a little more tame... but, he's not going to say no to trying a few things out.

"I've done threesomes before. You want to show her a good time?"

"That'd be cool, man... I'm new to this stuff. Besides, I don't think I like her on a dating level. I think I like someone with a little more personality. She's just fire," Aegan contemplates.

"Pfft... I know you ain't talkin," Julian laughs.

"Man... shut the fuck up," Aegan snorts.

Aegan is the free spirit on the floor. Everyone has seen him and Julian running through the halls naked, playing tricks on the others. Since the floors are gendered, there's nothing to really be concerned about. Aegan, Julian care about nothing other than being in the moment. You definitely know when they are back from a successful match on the pitch.

'Damn, put some clothes on!'
'What are we, toddlers?'

Some of the other guys on the hall are annoyed... but they are not finna learn if they can get Aegan to submit. He's jacked, as is Julian. They're surprised both are kind of subdued outside the dorm.

"I'on know 'what' you talmbout."

Aegan is one of the most charming guys on campus; even as a first year, he gets noticed. Until he receives his letter jacket for rugby, he walks around with his gear from Academy. Almost daring someone to pick on him for being "freshmeat."

A few of the frat boys invite him to events, already peeping his worth; but he declines. He has options... his dad's frat has a strong alumni base in Cali; Mr. Marlon, who pledged in undergrad, and Hannon, who crossed in grad school, are in the same frat. However, Aegan is very much like his mom in this respect: he won't pledge at all. That doesn't mean he won't go to the parties. Especially since some of his teammates are Greek.

Marcus and Roman talk and laugh about sports...
and politics... upcoming graduation... and colleges...
prepping the grill. Denae and Morocco, preparing a
few things in the kitchen while getting ready for the
cookout in the back.

   "Your dad's really smitten with him."

Bassel washes a few items then hands them to
Denae for cutting.

   "I like him too, mommy."

Morocco grabs a pan out of the fridge... a quiet
approval, but it's superfluous. Morocco will decide
Roman's place in his life.

Marcus' side of the family is in town to visit for a few
days. Roman definitely fits in, and they are all
enamored with how respectful and smart he is.
Marcus actually let him fire up the grill.

   "My dad goes to grill and smokehouse
   competitions all the time," Roman explains.

Always modest, giving respect to those who taught
him. He definitely takes pride in legacy-building.

   "I don't think he understands how big a deal it
   was for Sable to go to the playoffs in baseball.
   That hasn't happened in what... 30 years or
   something like that."

Roman is also big on history and milestones,
ignoring that the baseball team got swept in the first
round because of seeding. He is proud of that man:
his biggest cheerleader.

Morocco admits he is still growing on him...

   "And mom... he's like really attentive... like...

REALLY attentive," Morocco blushes a bit.

"I don't need to know EVERYTHING about that boy," Denae heads out the door, down to the grill.

Morocco stands at the top, proud of making the switch. Roman is stern, but gentle; guiding, but not directing; he's a star that lets others shine... and recognizes their luminance.

He's always known he likes dudes, and he allows Morocco to navigate that curiosity with him. He's much more secure than Lamar was.

"Where's Morocco?" Roman asks.

"Inside. Stay where folks' can see you," Denae commands.

"Yes ma'am. I mean... I'm not like that. I want something long-term with him, so anything is just under the assumption that I'm not leaving that boy any time soon."

They seem to know by now that Morocco and Roman have been intimate... a lot!

"So... you just gon' admit that right in front of everyone?"

Marcus sizes up Roman.

"No disrespect, but would it be any different if he or I were a girl... and one of us came up pregnant?"

Desmond laughs at his older brother being humbly checked... memories of his nephew come to mind.

"Morocco got himself a good one," he teases...

Marcus responds with a stern look.

"How'd y'all feel the first time you met Miss Marlon?" Roman asks.

Marcus concedes the point. They all loved Denae the moment they met her. She is charming, intelligent, ambitious, and comes from good people.

"So... you're Morocco's Denae?" Desmond smirks...

Marcus doesn't really like that.

"Well, as long as neither of you is me... we good!"

Marcus, not sure what he is trying to prove.

"What's wrong with being you?" Roman asks.

"He was a bit 'friendly' before he met his Denae," Desmond laughs.

"I'm gon' kick- your- fucking- ass!"

Marcus puts his glass down.

"Leave him alone!"

Mother Washington steps in, visiting temporarily.

"You always take his side!" Marcus huffs.

Roman sneaks away to spend some quiet time with Morocco.

"Hey lover... hey lover..." he serenades.

"I love you, too," Morocco swoons.

Marcus can't enjoy his meal at this restaurant. The thought of his son getting married... to a man... still a bit foreign for him. He's never had to deal with a... gay wedding? Eigan and Hanjoon didn't get married... Joey doesn't appear to be close to monogamy, let alone a proposal. Marcus is supportive, but this hits very close to home. It's the first time he's had to think about a gay man close to him getting married.

"I'm just waiting for him to graduate, sir."

Marcus chews over the proposal.

"I know I don't need your permission, I just need his... but I want no bad blood between us."

"Why do you want to get married to him?"

"I don't think marriage is for everyone, but it is for him and I. I want a record of my love for him in front of the universe and society. We get along very well, I just don't vibrate with anyone else. And I don't even want some flashy ceremony or a big deal to be made of this. I'm fine with he and I just going to the courthouse and walking off into the sunset. I love him, and he loves me."

It comforts Marcus because it sounds authentic, and consistent with who Roman is. Commitment is a big deal to him. He's not trying to do this as an affront to the conservatives; or to prove something to straight people who don't matter; or because he's 'always dreamed of having a (heteronormative) family.' No respectability politics here.

"Have you decided on school yet?"

"Well, as much as I would love to stay in Chi-town and be a wildcat... the bison are also pretty high on my list... but I've always wanted to honor my ancestors who served in segregated units. My dad doesn't think it's a good idea, but my aptitude is high enough I won't be in the field, especially if I go to Annapolis. Plebe summer starts end of June, but I'm considering staying here to be with your son."

"You have it all planned out," Marcus sips his cordial.

"But I also know plans must be adaptable."

Roman is consistently reasonable, and that is very reassuring to Marcus in a world that seems to be increasingly hostile to gay men again... and was already hostile to Black men.

"Well, there's probably one other person you might want to consider talking to... knows him better than anyone. And will likely be at any wedding you decide to plan... no matter how flashy it is or isn't going to be."

Marcus waves the waiter away from the table, declining another beverage.

* * * * *

Morocco knows where Roman is... just hoping to have his dad's blessing. For most of his life, marriage between two men has been a foreseeable dream. He's nervous as he sees the confident stride of Roman approaching the theatre.

"Hey!"

He embraces Morocco, combing his hair from his face.

"You seem very happy," Morocco fails to hide a smile.

"Yeah, your dad says he has some things to think about. He's ultimately not going to say no... but..."

Roman pauses.

Morocco steps back, anxious about this break in conversation.

"Well?"

"I didn't know you had another brother... Aegan?"

Roman tries to search Morocco's eyes, which begin to widen.

"Who told you about that? Man, fuck him!"

Morocco actually tampers his anger, believe it or don't.

"Well... your dad thinks it would be a good idea for me to meet him–"

"Then fuck you, too! You don't have to insert yourself into everything, Roman. It's complicated. And there's a lot of things Aegan doesn't understand. He–

Why am I even telling you any of this? That's MY family, not yours!"

"Yeah, but your dad–"

"Then date my dad... leave me the hell alone, Roman," Morocco storms off.

"Wait, what about the movie?"

Roman, confused on what the fuck just happened... watches Morocco storm off down the street... abandoning plans, not just for this evening. Tears stream down Roman's face, contradicting his stern countenance... as he watches his dream disappear into the night.

'Did he just break up with me? But... why? What did I do?'

Jesse calls Lamar...

"They broke up!"

Nosy ass was outside the theatre... saw the whole scene go down. But held on to this news until he was pretty sure... since neither Morocco or Roman are posting feigns.

"I couldn't tell, but I think Roman got too close to one of his brothers, or something..."

Jesse knows how Lamar feels about 'that Washington boy.'

Lamar sits on the info.

$\mathcal{L}$amar and MaryAnn have been going pretty strong for a while. He plans on taking this relationship into the school year. She weathers the "ain't he gay" detractions that attack her every moment of every day. She liked him from the moment they met... just bided her time, occasionally friendly, but always kind and present while playing the long game.

"He don't fuck like he gay," she responds to critiques that he doesn't know about.

Morocco refuses to speak to Roman... he owes him no explanation. He tried calling the house one-time to speak... and all Morocco said to him is "you got dumped... exes aren't supposed to keep in touch," then ended the call.

Roman let Morocco block him from his life.

"Why are you taking it out on him? He's allowed to be surprised," Denae shakes her head.

"Blame dad for making this about Aegan... Roman is not my boyfriend, y'all need to come to terms with that. Lamar and I might get back together."

Morocco weaponizes the revelation without looking at his mother.

"You need to stop bouncing between relationships... it's obvious to those of us who know... that you miss Aegan," Denae coaxes.

"Of course I miss him... and he would adore Roman. I just feel like part of me chose him subconsciously because Aegan WOULD like him. But I need to stop making decisions for Aegan. I need to make my own decisions. Roman just isn't the one, mom."

"Um hmmm..."

Denae brushes Morocco's hair. He wants braids now. Not really a style typical for this family, but 'at least he isn't doing dreadlocks.'

"You think Aegan hates Lamar?" She breaks the silence.

"I know Aegan hates Lamar," Morocco rolls his

eyes.

"Do you know why?"

"It doesn't matter why he hates Lamar: that's my man! He doesn't ask me about his girlfriends," Morocco dismisses.

"What girlfriends?"

As if Morocco would know. Besides, Aegan has not really been known to date.

* * * * *

Morocco stands in the open area, admiring his new look in a handheld mirror, listening to his parents arguing. Marcus defends Aegan against Morocco.

"I don't give a fuck about how that boy feel... that's MY son! I'm sick of whatever this is between them two, and it needs to stop!"

"That's not your decision, Marcus. Let that boy figure some things out on his own. You wrong as hell for telling Roman about Aegan."

Marcus sucks his teeth...

"How I'm 'posed to know he don't even talk about-"

He turns in the direction where Morocco can hear him more clearly...

"-his own damn best friend!"

Morocco storms up the stairs to his room... and slams the door.

"You don't own no fucking doors in here!"

Denae grabs Marcus' arm... stopping him from charging up the stairs.

"I'm gon' hurt that boy one day... and you need to stop stopping me."

Marcus looks at Denae.

"Oh... this what we doing today?"

She lets go and steps back... sizing up Marcus.

He thinks twice... waves his hands in the air...

"Awww..."

...and goes downstairs to play with his other sons.

* * * * *

It felt like a long summer. Everyday was a new activity, but that was intentional. Morocco added a summer baseball season with the city league, which almost conflicted with hosting a booth during pride week. Lamar has been traveling with his own summer ball, so they have hardly seen each other. He misses him so much.

"How are you holding up?"
Morocco whimpers on the phone.

"I'm kind of sick of travel, but I still want to stay in shape. Who knows, maybe I'll try out for the team this year. Coach hasn't really asked me, not sure why."

"I can't wait to come see you play, 'cause I know you're going to make the team," Morocco encourages.

"I'on know about all that, man, like... we don't need to be all up on each other like that... do we?"

"Lamar, I'm not going to accost you on the

court. I just want to watch you play."

Morocco rolls his eyes.

"Yeah, but you make my dick hard... so that might be a bit of a distraction... you remember how I hurt my arm," Lamar laughs.

Morocco is annoyingly familiar with the story.

"You come see me play, what's the big deal?"

"I am still working through some things, man, be easy!"

Lamar needs to get off the phone so he can suit up. Teammates are filing in, and he doesn't want them to know why he is a bit aroused right now.

"Well, when do you get back?"

They were supposed to be spending more time together, but those plans haven't panned out.

It almost feels like Lamar joined the amateur team for two reasons: one, he got tired of hearing about Sable's baseball team, and two... he doesn't know how to let MaryAnn down in person.

He gave himself a built-in excuse, but Morocco doesn't mind: he loves Lamar... and it almost feels like a husband coming home. Marcus doesn't like this dynamic, but who cares! It's not his life.

He really loved playing baseball, getting regional honorable mention. He clipped the articles from the paper, placing them it in a little pile with other stories featuring him... especially the one reviewing his appearance with the Windy City Ballet Company. Lamar was at that performance... surprising him with flowers delivered to the dressing room on opening and closing night.

Plenty of space in Lamar's place for practicing, so it's like he has his own personal dance studio. Lamar likes him as a dancer... but not necessarily as a baseball player, to an extent. Maybe both, definitely not over dance.

'I wonder why,' Morocco occasionally has a passing thought, facing a conflict of existence.

* * * * *

Sable feels a lot more relaxed this year. No dating drama: questions or solicitations. He wears Lamar's Academy letter jacket for basketball; and since everyone knows his name is Morocco, it's about the clearest signal he can send that rejects any thoughts of rendering this asunder.

As if junior year won't he hard enough with graduation tests next semester, he's being tasked with choreo for a musical in February and teaching a new piece for the spring showcase.

   "Is Mr. Alvin insane?"

Not because Morocco can't do it, but because he'd rather not. The price of being good. How is he going to balance that with winter baseball workouts?! And he also has at least five solo improvs to submit by the end of the semester... plus the band has a tour over winter break. And then there's college applications and visits... and there's a scout coming for fall ball!

And now... Hyun's starting to expect Morocco to be a big brother. He's avoiding Marcus; Hannon is too old; and Aegan's out of reach.

"Like... how do you know you like someone?"

Hyun gets a quiet moment with Morocco.

"Are you already... like...?"

"Maybe, but I don't feel comfortable talking to you about that. I mean... isn't it different?"

"I don't know, I've never been attracted to girls."

Morocco feels a bit inadequate to answer questions; he can sense that Hyun believes he is not qualified... just available.

"And I'm not attracted to guys."

Hyun, head bowed, waits for some kind of straw to grasp. He loves his brother, but... who can he run to? No one else, right now.

Morocco pauses.

"All I can say is that... you don't necessarily have to worry about being physically harmed for your attraction. So take that for what it's worth. You're not shy for any reason, you know exactly what you like and you go for it. Are there any girls at school who really interest you?"

"No, but everyone has a girlfriend... and their girlfriends all want me. So there's this pressure that I don't really want right now. I hear the rumors on campus... and a lot of them are going to be going to Academy next year. It's this girl at Sable who's been featuring me... but how do I know that's not because she can't get with you?"

"First of all, it's ok to not have a girlfriend. Since when are you victim to peer pressure?"

"Morocco... I'm already having dreams... my body's changing... maybe later than everyone else... but it is. I mean... we all know when you started," Hyun informs.

"How– you know what... nevermind. I used to catch Hannon all the time... and dad has a 'pre-mom' reputation. So, it's ok to not want to settle down... it runs in our family. I'm just lucky that I found a guy I really like," Morocco smiles.

"I liked Roman... he knows you really well! But I can see why you go for Lamar... no homo," Hyun smirks.

Morocco, a little shocked that his brother pays that much attention...

"Oh, you think you know me?"

Hyun tosses his rugby ball, leaning on the door frame.

"I know you're reserved, and not reckless. But then I hear you used to be really good at rugby, until you fell in love with baseball. So, it's ok to switch it up... when you change your mind, it's for a good reason, I guess."

Morocco isn't sure what his brother is trying to say about him.

"I have work to do..."

He looks at some of his costume sketches.

"I couldn't do baseball... and that's ok,

Morocco; I love you for being different and unexpected."

Hyun turns and heads to the staircase... pausing outside of Aegan's room... before sneaking past his parents' door to head downstairs.

Morocco rips up his renderings...

"I don't like those outfits, I need a new concept..."

He abandons his drafting desk for his bed.

*I*t's a quiet night outside of Tainted. Patrons choose more daylight excursions and less hidden destinations... as a rise in homophobia hits the most accepting areas of Berkeley. The local gay community center has already seen an increase in vandalism, not to mention the demands that it be closed coming from within the LGBT community... you know, those respectability gays who believe assimilation is freedom.

Protests and rallies on campus increased the appearance of the straight crowds in the bar... which scared away the gays... leaving only a few pockets of attendees once the 'allies' felt it was "safe enough" to return to their own watering holes and let the gays have their space again.

The danger returned: for those who want to ensure Tainted stays open... they must now re-navigate those who seek trouble. And the protests aren't coming back any time soon... the 'allies' feel like they have done enough for now.

Though his skin color did not protect him from being a target of these men who share his skin color, Jesse is not scared... The 'phobes can't keep him from living his authentic life.

The apps aren't where he feels connected; he prefers to meet his desires face-to-face; but perhaps he should select those daytime destinations on the main strip... and forget about the locales that honor traditional gay life... you know, the kind those aforementioned respectability gays want to avoid, and hope are eventually shutdown.

   "Whatcha doing down here, faggot?"

Jesse refuses to live in fear. He's from Chi-town. His other college friends, too scared to continue going to bars, stay in relationships with toxic men because it is safer than the possibility that they could be beaten to death... a reality that faces Jesse in this moment.

A group of boys begins shoving our queen, whose only weapon is a sharp tongue encouraging these "family values, 'christian' men of supremacy" to do their worst... a mouth that refuses to scream in terror... and a body that believes the sun won't see breathe again.

One of the boys begins to choke... a sound that distracts the other four, as they cease their assault on someone who appeared to be without protection. The audacity of these two strange guys... to defend this faggot cowering on the grime of the alleyway... one of whose hands are a vice on their buddy. Unsure of their next move, Jesse regains his senses and, knowing the male anatomy well... punches with all his might. Another one of the four 'phobes standing above him doubles over in pain.

As the group seeks to retreat opposite our two allies, a third appears to block their way. They are not outnumbered... but they quickly realize they are out-manned. They drop their weapons to surrender.

But surrender won't be allowed on this night. Though no death will occur... though some gay man somewhere; some lesbian somewhere; some trans somewhere... may succumb to an assault in this modern era... it won't be at the hands of these assailants, as our four will make sure that these 'phobes won't be allowed to harm another... without remembering this night.

Our third charges the group... tackling one of our guilty party to the ground.

Morocco sneaks into the home... disabling the security system... if not his mother's curiosity, pending his ability to slide past her room to the safest most dangerous room he knows. 'He don't run shit no more.'

He tries his best to ignore the eventual bruises on his skin, the tingling from missing hairs on the side of his head... as he wonders why the trophy under his fingernails does not feel like a victory.

He finds the card collection: pristine, each collectible has its place... each printed piece of cardboard its own sleeve. He knows the value of what he has in his possession... forget an appraisal, it won't be high enough.

He knows that might be too much... and leaves the innocent victims alone, but he has to send a message. He closes the book, and falls asleep with it instead.

The smell of his mother jars him from his slumber.

"Leave me alone, ma," he commands.

Denae won't fight him. She sees the cuts on his face, bloodied knuckles; and the skin under his nails indicates he was not nearly as helpless as that encounter makes him feel in this moment. He cannot let his brothers see him injured, feeling weak alongside them... weak through no fault of his upbringing.

"I fell trying to do the new routine, ma."

He lies to a person who he believes he can deceive.

She takes the card collection from him.

"There are easier ways to commit suicide than

this," she warns him.

"I wish he would try," Morocco issues an idle threat.

Denae gives a monotone reply, a single syllable... weighted with 'no, you don't.'

She replies in kind...

"You want to file a police report?"

"I already told you what happened!"

It's the most respectful 'no' he wants to give at this time. What makes her think she can fight all his battles? Who does she think she is?

"You have school today..." Denae leaves the room.

He sneaks into this room often; sometimes in admiration, sometimes in jealousy... but rarely removes anything from its place...

"There are easier ways to commit suicide..."

He scans the trophies... the accolades... the articles pinned on the walls... and that's not even taking inventory of his skills on the pitch. Even in music... no way Morocco could attend the Academy... the comparisons would have been non-existent... and, the underachieving, too apparent. What better way to outshine this room than to focus on a path HE would have never taken: not because he wasn't qualified... he just didn't want to take it.

"I hate him so much!"

Morocco whispers to himself, finishing up in the bathroom... already knowing he won't make the opening bell. At least, at this school, he doesn't have to worry about seeing or hearing his name anywhere.

Lamar catches Morocco outside of his first session... wanting a kiss.

"Where were you this morning?" He asks.

Morocco ignores his boyfriend, walking right on past him. Not intentional, just has his mind on being attacked last night... for simply existing. Lamar grabs his arm, startling him... he almost swings.

"Hey, what did I do?" Lamar ducks.

As his senses return, Lamar sees a few scratches on the flawless face of the boy he loves. His hair is down today, easier to cover any scratches or bruises that may form during the school hours. He grabs his hands... chipped fingernails that tell a story Morocco won't reveal any time soon. Lamar steps away, being repelled by a stern grimace demanding that he 'not see me like this.' His own internal battles also assist the retreat.

First session needed to be missed... too many people. 'Calculus, at a performing arts school, no less!' His grades are fine, he will graduate with top honors... just like his predecessors. It's not that he cannot defend himself: he has. Even at a fine arts school... there are homophobes and bullies. But, on the cusp of manhood, he begins to realize the world tomorrow will be quite different from the world in these halls. He wants to say something to Lamar... but Lamar cannot solve this issue. His love is not enough in this moment, for some reason, it's–

Morocco falls to the floor.

"Mr. Washington, where is your mind today? That is a simple spin... where are you spotting? You have missed it every run-through we've done!"

Mr. Alvin scolds his pupil, a repeated scene this morning, but Morocco has tuned out.

Maybe today was not a good day to come to school. Maybe he should have just stayed at Lamar's place last night; he doesn't have classes today, he would not have cared if Morocco slept over. That's part of the reason Lamar got his own place, so they could spend more time together. It's worth getting in trouble over... he loves Lamar. But this is exactly what concerned his mother.

'It's her fault. She shouldn't be giving me a curfew!'

His solo hour is over... now other dancers file in.

"Just two more hours," he mumbles to himself.

It's an easy senior year, as the only real obstacle left to hurdle is the winter showcase. The Solar System will be the focus of this year's program, and the community has already sold out a few of the shows.

Each senior contemporary dancer will represent a planet, except when they get to Jupiter. All dancers will participate in that piece, which will feature Morocco. For some reason, today... he recalls a senior-year concert at the Academy from a few years back... where someone else performed Jupiter... and–

"I swear, Morocco!"

He missed his entrance... and his mark... and forgot the new blocking...

"OUT!"

Mr. Alvin shortens the amount of time left in the first half of his school day.

Morocco leaves campus altogether, sending an alert to Marcus' phone... who calls his son... and gets sent to voicemail... while Morocco walks over to the train... heading down to "The Loop."

*   *   *   *   *

He waits in the lobby as the security guards make phone calls. A concierge walks over to him.

"Take these elevators up to the 77th floor."

The concierge winks at him as he scans his badge on a security gate... Morocco blushes. The gate swings and an open elevator door waits for him to enter. The concierge presses a button.

"Let me know if you need anything," he offers.

Morocco, with a sheepish "thanks," brushes his hair from his face.

The panel numbers start at 50. As Morocco can almost feel the elevator move on a smooth ride within the column... his mind wanders for two reasons. He is curious to see what the space looks like now that the business appears to be doing very well. He also hopes to stave off his dad's anger, if he can use this visit as an excuse.

The receptionist, wondering if the company's boss has a twin or a child, asks Morocco who he is here to see.

"Hannon."

The boldness of this visitor to just call him by first name! The receptionist reaches out her hand.

"I'm sorry, he is in a meeting right now. First, I need your name, and you'll likely have to wait until he is done."

The office continues to buzz around them, with a lot of excitement and purpose. He hands her his ID, and a crimson light flashes on her console. She knows what that means. It's a simple notification system they made for this office where the top team has a list of special guests who get to bypass usual security protocols.

She turns to another person behind the desk.

"I'll be back... Mr. Washington, follow me."

As Morocco walks through the office, it feels too laid back. Basketball hoops on desks; ping pong; TVs showing movies and even a group playing video games in a corner. The views of Chicago are spectacular, though: that should be reason enough to come to work.

"Give me a moment..."

The receptionist taps a card to the door. As it opens, what was frosted glass now becomes clear. Morocco gasps.

"That's so cool!"

"It's done with water vapor; a security feature, while important meetings and phone calls are being held," the receptionist informs.

"No meeting is more important than you,

though, Morocco."

Hannon walks over and hugs his brother.

"Thanks, Stephanie. I am glad to see that setup works well!"

You can hear how proud Hannon is of what he and his friends from college have accomplished... smart investments and contracts notwithstanding.

"Nah, we don't call ourselves executives or leadership. We're workshopping a few terms, but we don't need folks being on pins and needles when we walk past. Everyone is going to ask who you are, though. I can introduce you if you–"

"I got kicked out of school today," Morocco lies.

Hannon pauses.

"You're not that type of kid... what's wrong?"

Morocco shows him his hand... and Hannon notices his nails are chipped and unkempt.

"Why have you been fighting?"

"I didn't have a choice, and now I can't concentrate on anything. I don't want to talk about it... let's go do something," Morocco evades, fighting a tear or two.

Hannon begins to offer...

"Mom and dad–"

"Are you going to be a brother or a fucking parent!?"

Morocco does not want any suggestions at this

time.

Hannon calls one of his business partners...

"Yeah, I can handle the rest of the day. That call this morning was the best news ever! We about to be rich-er!" Ammar laughs.

As they exit the office, everyone now knows the company news, and the crowd gives Hannon a standing ovation. He fans his arms, almost like his days hyping up the basketball crowds in college. Morocco slowly walks behind his brother, taking in the moment. He remembers those days, not that long ago. Hannon has always been the standard.

'I wonder if these people truly know who they're working for.'

On a quieter floor of the company, Morocco shoots a little pool with his brother. They don't get to talk too much. The years between them aside, Hannon has been building a life of his own trying to bring more tech to Chi-town. They don't text each other a lot... not because they can't... just, they're not as close as... well, we don't have to talk about him.

"How you like my old room?" Hannon leans on a wall.

"I kind of live with Lamar now. But it's pretty cool how much stuff mom and dad put in there for you. I guess that's going to be the thing, next one up gets your old room."

"That might have been the intention, until—"

"I don't want to talk about him. He always trying to outshine everyone and do his own damn thing. Fuck him!"

"Morocco... what's this really about, man? You've been mad at him for years now, and no one knows why."

Hannon tries to console.

"He knows what he did."

Morocco dismisses.

"I'm not sure he does. But I am guessing your nails have something to do with it?"

"When's the last time grampa came up?" Morocco changes the topic.

"He can't make the trip anymore. That last travel took a lot out of him. I am glad he was here, though. Part of the reason this company exists is because of him and his civil rights work. Bias in tech is a thing, and with A.I. making videos and pictures using all sorts of human imaging, it is important that racism does not play a factor in how Black people are portrayed."

"You're so smart"

Morocco smiles.

"Not as smart as–"

"Fuck him!"

Morocco pouts.

"Our mom! Calm down, man. You need to process that: he is not your enemy. Never has been! Damn, you as bad as Joey used to be... with none of the trauma!"

Hannon gets annoyed.

"He still single? I'd date him if Lamar wasn't in the picture," Morocco giggles.

"Man... leave my friends alone! He used to do that shit all the time. I don't think he would ever date any of us, even if that were a possibility. He would not want to damage the bond that we all have with him. He is more like a brother than you may realize."

"When are we going to become guncles?"

Hannon laughs the question away... as his phone rings.

Marcus shouts...

"Find your brother, I think he done lost his got-damn mind–"

"He's here with me, dad."

Marcus pauses...

"Let me speak to him. This boy done gon' crazy... skipping school, not answering MY calls!"

Hannon looks at Morocco.

"Let me be a brother today, dad."

It calms Marcus, for the moment. He sighs...

"You can't replace him."

"I'm not trying to, never want to," Hannon cools his dad.

"Tell him he better be home for dinner... no Lamar tonight!" Marcus ends the call.

Morocco stares out over the skyline, assuming his brother's response.

"I'll tell him you stayed with me."

Hannon tries to buffer... especially since Morocco has hidden a lot of Hannon's secrets.

"We should probably make that statement the truth... I don't want to talk to Lamar right now: I feel so ugly."

Hannon, at a loss for words, the two play a few more games to clear the afternoon.

Jesse walks across campus... rushing to class. Maybe picking up a few shifts at Tainted wasn't a good idea, but he feels so much safer and validated in being gay... in lieu of recent events. A group of boisterous rugby boys make their way across campus. For whatever reason, Jesse feels cautious, but safe around them.

One looks at him and nods his head, but the rest of the group largely ignores him. They holler ahead of them to "A-Dub," and Jesse gets a little aroused... pausing in his tracks.

"Good god... that's a specimen!"

He remarks out loud, as Miranda walks up.

"You should stay away from the athletes, don't you think?"

"I don't know... they are men, I am gay, what you want me to say?"

"They would break you in half!"

"And that's not a bad thing... correct?"

They laugh.

"We should go to their games," he suggests...

More salacious thoughts being the prevailing motive. That nod from one of the players was NO mistake.

It's been a few weeks, and Morocco is still acting out, not willing to talk with anyone about what happened that night.

"You have never struck me as the type of kid to be apprehensive. I think that's what Lamar feeds off of you."

Dr. Barnes, taking note of a Morocco who has become reserved, as he leaves campus one day... almost successful in avoiding her... better at avoiding Lamar.

This semester is a complete anomaly from everything Morocco has built before and during his time at Sable. He won't be eligible to play baseball in the spring if his grades decline, let alone his recent attendance issues. Election season is not helping him at all.

Marcus and Denae have never been aggressive parents with any of their children... let alone Morocco, who has always been the most loving and lovable. As they walk the halls of the performing arts school... leaving a parent-teacher meeting with Mr. Alvin...

"Mr. and Mrs. Washington?"

The couple turns to see a former schoolmate of their oldest sons.

"Hi, Stanley... you teaching or something?"

"Well, yes; I am doing a work-study program as I get my certification. There were no teaching assistant positions on campus... so I worked something out here. I didn't realize you contributed to Sable."

"Morocco goes here. We just left a meeting with one of his teachers."

"Oh, I haven't seen him around campus at all. He's not taking any science courses?"

"It's his last year, he fulfilled all his science with some of the summer programs. Physics with calculus would have been the only science he would have been eligible to take. Since it's not required, he chose to take Cal2 instead. Says it's easy, though he didn't want to be good in math." Denae explains.

"Why not?" Stanley is just as confused.

"He wants to form his own path... which is part of the reason he transferred here after you all graduated."

Marcus gives a more succinct reply, slightly protecting his son.

"Has Aegan been back to Chicago? I keep telling him to hit me up when he's in town."

"Not even for the holidays. I think he just wanted to get away from a lot of things here. Boy been fighting other people's bullies since he was a kid. He went to Cali for kind of a quieter life, I guess," Marcus assumes.

"Nah... he went to Cali because he wanted a challenge. He almost couldn't get from under Hannon's shadow... even though, in many ways... he did," Stanley corrects.

"Well... now you know why Morocco transferred. He was always going to do something in the arts. Academy has an impressive list, but nothing like Sable. We are not shocked he got in. But he's off this year for some reason. And I don't think it's senior jitters."

Marcus squeezes Denae's arm, telling her she's talking too much; she slaps his hand away.

"Has he seen Morocco perform?" Stanley inquires.

"It's been a while..."

Marcus checks his watch.

"Don't forget to stop by the house, the boys would love to see you. When's the wedding?" Denae asks.

"We're not sure yet, there's a lot of schedules to plan around. My fiancé is from San Fran, so it works out for us. I'll be sure to get you two an invite," Stanley offers.

"We'd like that."

Denae and Marcus head out.

Stanley gives one of his groomsmen a phone call.

The scrum-half is distracted for some reason... practice wasn't smooth all week, and this game didn't look crisp. Jesse thinks it may be because he was flirting a little with one of the ruggers.

"Nah, he's cool. We have a pretty proud legacy of gay players on this team. One fought back on 9/11 and one of his teammates got assassinated with his partner about ten years ago. You've seen the clips of that really popular gay activist who used to always get called before Congressional committees? I think he also played rugby, but I forgot where he went to school. None of the ruggers care about me being open..."

Nathan answers Jesse... who correctly pegged the nod he was given a few weeks back.

"I feel like I know him... like he's familiar for some reason..."

Jesse senses an energy from three of Nathan's teammates... cooling after a hard-fought game, eeking out a close home victory.

"That would be interesting. Like... I didn't think he went that way–"

"No... not familiar like that, just... I can't put my finger on it..."

Jesse dismisses it...

"Anyway, one of my friends back home is getting married..."

...walking off with Nathan, who has abandoned post-game celebrations to find out about this cute guy who kept showing up to games and practices...

staring at him.

* * * * *

Aegan and Julian watch a few highlight reels at the team house. Julian lays on Aegan, as the two are on the couch. The visiting team has left, so the ruggers can relax among themselves.

"See, right there... I told you: you missed the gap," Julian points at the screen. "Scrummy in!"

He throws up his hands in frustration.

"Aww... no one cares," Aegan dismisses.

"Hoe, you almost cost us the game!"

"We won, didn't we? Fuck you mean!" Aegan dismisses the critique.

"Damn, y'all look gay as fuck," one of the teammates tries to joke.

"Not my fault no one likes touching you, Ram. Not even that doll in your room feels safe. When you replace it with one of those new life-like versions, you'll learn that no means no... even from artificial intelligence."

Aegan points at the TV about to criticize Julian... who shoos his hand away.

"Exactly!"

He ignores the other guys ribbing the hooker; Ram doesn't care, he knows his own business.

Julian knows a lot of Aegan's secrets, and Aegan knows a lot of Julian's secrets. Julian being the name Hanjoon used to use to fit in... is purely coincidental. Both of them used to terrorize the bullies when they went to school together. And they competed with each other throughout school, even if at a distance. Julian graduated with a slightly higher GPA... Aegan got more national recognition on the pitch. Both are "who's who" caliber.

"So... how did the date go?"

Julian waits for Aegan to fully get back inside.

"Really well, like... oh man... she's amazing! Just what I am looking for. She wants to see me again..."

"She knows you're not a virgin?"

"Yeah, but she doesn't care. She said most people want to get it out the way in college, and she was impressed I had waited so long."

The two laugh.

"Good, man... I'm not ready to get married yet. But... um... I think I'm about to be a dad!" Julian discloses.

"Oh, shit! That's awesome man, does anyone else know?"

"Only if she told someone," Julian considers.

"Well, now I feel bad not telling you this. I wasn't sure how you would react. She and I did it the night we met– "

"So... what are you saying? You nutt quick?" Julian laughs.

Aegan smiles... giving Julian a little shove.

BERKELEY HAS A LOADED ROSTER... LED BY AN ALL-AMERICAN.

Coach calls a team meeting... as they are waiting to hear back from a school that had to postpone a match earlier in the season.

"It's an important game, but if they lose to us here, they won't make the playoffs. They need a few other things to happen... then they can avoid playing us, but still get in. It might not be worth the risk to bring their team to town. You might want the rest... but I am working on a scrimmage... so you boys don't get soft on me. Keep 'em all scared of ya!"

Morocco lays in bed, Lamar's arm across his chest as only one of them appears to be awake... mind wandering. He scrolls through a few posts on his phone, looking at a few pictures from that spring concert not so long ago.

"Of all the pieces to be doing for my senior year... it has to be the one he did his senior year."

Morocco mumbles as he stares at the band in the picture.

Some legacies, you just cannot escape... no matter what you do, or how hard you try to change your path.

Lamar stirs.

"I should probably go..."

Morocco has enough on his plate without antagonizing his parents. While the sun is still out... he will safely avoid multiple repeat encounters.

"You want me to walk with you? Apparently there have been a few more attacks."

"Then how would you get back and safe?"

"I'm not worried about that. I'm kind of glad I was able to get a position at your school... I care about you. I don't want anything to happen to you. I'm not trying to be your protector or anything–"

"Good! Cause I can take care of myself!"

Morocco proceeds to leave.

Lamar, unintentionally agitating his boyfriend, but not sure why the idea of needing protection upsets him. It was never about what... but always about who. And the protector he *thinks* he needs... is no longer around.

Lamar, scrolling his phone...

"Hey... Jesse's dating a rugby player now!"

Morocco rolls his eyes.

"My boyfriend says he knows you..."

Nathan corners A-Dub after practice one day.

"I've seen him around campus a few times. That's about it."

A-Dub takes a sip of water as they walk past the stadium, towards the sunset.

"Oh... I thought maybe you knew each other from Chicago or something. I didn't think Sable had a rugby team."

Nathan continues phishing, wondering if his teammate has 'my man' on his mind.

"They don't..."

A-Dub's thoughts change: a man is definitely on his mind... a man who chose a school that didn't have a rugby team.

"They have baseball, tennis, hockey... but it's a really good performing arts school. What else you know about Sable?"

"Oh... nothing... I think they're going through some of the same stuff we were enduring for a few weeks. I am grateful Jesse didn't get caught up in some of those attacks here: I really like him."

Nathan wants to ask without asking. He feels like he is getting closer to his answer. A-Dub and Julian are so close, and he's never given Nathan any grief about being gay. He helped Nathan come out... so it would only make sense.

"Hmmm... Jesse looks like he can take care of himself. Most gay men can... what's that got to do with Sable?"

"He says one of the star dancers got assaulted a few weeks back and hasn't been dealing with the aftermath too well..."

A-Dub stops in his tracks.

A SUSPECT HAS BEEN IDENTIFIED IN A STRING OF UNSOLVED ATTACKS AROUND BOYSTOWN... YOU MIGHT REMEMBER A FEW NIGHTS AGO, WE TOLD YOU ABOUT A MAN WHO HAS BEEN BEATEN INTO A COMA... WE SHOWED YOU HIS PICTURE. WELL... ACCORDING TO YOU, OUR VIEWERS... THAT MAN HAS A HISTORY OF HARASSING AND ASSAULTING SEVERAL PEOPLE AROUND THE GAY BARS UP AND DOWN NORTH HALSTED. POLICE SAY THEY ARE INVESTIGATING TO SEE IF THERE IS ANY TRUTH TO THIS... CONFIRMING THEY HAVE RECEIVED AN INCREASE IN PHONE CALLS RELATED TO THIS NOW SUSPECT... IDENTIFYING HIM IN THOSE ASSAULTS... SOME REPORTED, AND OTHERS NOW FILING REPORTS. WE WILL BE FOLLOWING THIS CASE... IF YOU HAVE ANY INFORMATION, CALL OUR NEWSROOM OR SEND US AN ANONYMOUS TIP VIA OUR WEBSITE AND SOCIAL MEDIA PAGES...

"Awww... the only reason they're interested in the case is because it's some straight, white man in the hospital. When it was random gays getting beat up, they didn't care."

Marcus opens the newspaper.

Morocco turns off the TV... puts on his headphones... and drifts away. Breakfast is over on a quiet Saturday morning. His siblings run downstairs for their own various activities, as he needs space to practice his routine. He cannot hear the doorbell, and does not notice his mother leave the room.

Denae opens the front door... with a look of unhappy pleasure on her face. She sighs... rolls her eyes... not even going to attempt an argument at this time... she points upstairs.

Morocco marks a few steps and dance moves in the living room, headphones in... ignoring the rest of the world as preparation for this showcase continues to dim his light. It's the simple things he continues to forget... the meticulous details that got him this far... now abandoning him.

He senses something... a pull... the energy in the house has changed, and he is not sure why. He turns towards the kitchen... and sees–

Anger displaces concentration... as he runs over to the man watching him practice. Marcus sits, 'not reading' the newspaper he holds in his hands... as Morocco begins to punch the impenetrable.

"Why the fuck are *you* here?"

He swings, while dodging hands that are not responding.

"You think I am not man enough or something?"

His target remains unphased... silent. Denae returns to sit by Marcus... ignoring the scene.

"Take your ass on back to Cali... no one wants you here!"

Morocco slaps Aegan.

"You're supposed to be dancing!"

...are the only words that stop Morocco.

"You need me to show you how to do that too?"

Morocco attempts to grab his brother's hair and pull him down... getting the response he thinks he wants.

Aegan hems Morocco up, slamming him to the wall, pinning him... the thump echoes in the large room. Marcus looks up from his paper, not really expecting this... knowing who his son is... ready to pretend he can stop him. Aegan's respect for his dad would be the only brakes that would work, as he hears the paper rattle behind him. It calms his response.

"Who the fuck are you?"

Aegan shames his brother.

"I am not who you left behind... that's for sure!"

"Keep lying to yourself and this will go all night. You're playing weak right now... and you never had that permission... from yourself... and damn sure not from me."

"I'm not you, Aegan."

"No one ever said you had to be, Roc. Mom? Dad? Hannon? Gram-ma? Who said you had to be me?"

Morocco begins to cry... he wails... loudly... startling Denae, as Marcus remains silent.

Steps attempt to announce curious children... to which Aegan orders:

"Stay down until I say otherwise."

Hearing the voice they know means business... they retreat quickly.

Marcus laughs...

"You ain't got no games coming up?"

Aegan ignores his dad... relaxing on Morocco... who squeezes him tightly... but Aegan cannot hug him just yet, will not hug him just yet. That does not matter to Morocco... feeling his brother's presence renews his resolve.

"Who told you?" Morocco weeps.

"Why does that matter? The real question is why did I need to be told," Aegan corrects.

"I asked you a question," Marcus reminds his son.

"We rescheduled, their team had a conflict."

Aegan continues allowing his brother to release his shame as he responds to their father.

"When are you heading back?" Denae asks.

"I don't know," Aegan answers.

"Go back now... no one needs you here!"

Morocco's words betray his actions.

"Then let go."

He just needs to feel his brother's energy... a few more minutes. Aegan never gets tired of being dependable.

Morocco suddenly lets go... then storms out of the house.

"Where's he going?" Aegan inquires.

"To the fun one... Hannon's always been the fun brother, you've always been the pillar. You already know that..."

Denae turns the page... as Marcus shoots her a glance and rolls his eyes: he wasn't finished reading!

"I can have fun, too."

"They don't need to see that side of you," she cautions.

Marcus scans some national news...

"Attacks to the LGBT community are on the decline in Berkeley. Interesting... you know anything about that?"

No reply from Aegan. Husband and wife share a quiet exchange...

"Wait... when did you get in town?"

Denae rhetorically asks, as her mind wanders to the suspect in a coma. Aegan walks towards the staircase.

"Sometimes I wonder if we named him after the wrong person," Marcus turns the page himself this time.

Denae smiles... "but just like his namesake... he struggles with lying."

Aegan calls downstairs...

"Where y'all at?"

...to which a stampede of feet respond, tackling their brother to the ground. Aegan takes note of the twins... thinking about an upcoming addition to the family.

Hyun is getting big, starting to fill out his frame. He wants to show his brother some of his tapes, wavering between playing flanker and wing at The Academy. He's versatile like that... his skills would get wasted for either position.

"I'm going to break your record!"

Aegan minimizes the bravado:

"Stick to poaching," he teases.

* * * * *

Morocco, still in the front yard as time feels like it creeps past. He wants to run to Hannon, but knows he should stay and talk to Aegan. There's a lot he does not know about him, he's always been private.

Aegan stares out the study at his brother, frozen in time, leaning on the front gate listening through his headphones... and leaves out the back of the house to avoid disturbing him.

He makes his way to Daddy Halsted's. He doesn't really even like pizza, but Morocco does... so he found this restaurant in the gayborhood and he and 'Roc' would often shoot the shit while Morocco eyes boys and flirts a little. 'I wonder if he still goes here.'

They make a mean sub sandwich: meat and cheese sliced to order... lettuce... tomatoes... pickle slices... onions... just a little mustard... oil, vinegar, salt, pepper, oregano.

"What type of bread?"

"Rosemary, thanks. Let me get the frozen sprite."

"We're out... you don't want to try the milkshakes?"

"Nah... lactose don't like me."

Aegan sits down... waiting for his order to be delivered. An energy in the room changes, and in walks a tall, dark-skinned man... either attending a military school, or has an interesting taste in clothes and haircuts.

"Let me get a 12 inch supreme... add Black olives–"

"Extra mushrooms, extra pepperoni..."

Aegan, remembering a familiar order, thought he whispered.

The man at the counter turns...

"Um... that actually sounds good, let me do that."

The man stares at Aegan. Aegan is not paying attention, just thinking about life.

As the man waits for his order, he takes a seat.

"Not sure I've ever seen you in here before," the guy greets.

"Oh, I don't live in Chicago anymore, I'm out west in college. Had to come back to handle some grown folks' business..."

Aegan pauses.

"Oh, nice... yeah, I am heading back to Annapolis in a bit myself. Just... this place reminds me of a lot of things."

He forces a smile of remembrance. The cashier brings Aegan his sandwich.

"Yeah, my brother loves to come here. I started bringing him here once I knew he was gay. It's his favorite restaurant. so it's kind of my favorite restaurant. He likes pizza; I don't."

"You're an exception," the man laughs.

Then, he reminisces...

"I met someone special in here. I think about

him a lot when I'm in town, but I had to get away when we broke up. I miss him so much."

"Eh, men are shitty. I'm about to raise one, though," Aegan confesses, feeling surprisingly comfortable.

"What's a straight-boy doing in this place?" the guy wrenches his face.

"Good food is good food. Besides, few places in the area make a better sandwich," Aegan slurps and slops the juicy sub.

The two sit and talk for a little while, losing track of time. Surprisingly, not mentioning where they went to prep school. As Aegan stands to exit, the guy rises as well... they bump shoulders... and Roman responds to Aegan's closeness... with a stare of admiration.

"No... I'm not attracted to men, but you good stock," Aegan confirms.

"I didn't think you were, you just remind me so much of some–"

The guy fights back a tear, no need to show too much vulnerability to this stranger. If our military man paid attention, Aegan's dark skin would reveal a lot; but the stranger is very distracted in the moment, his heart longs to beat again.

"Your ex? He liked olives, extra mushrooms and pepperoni?" Aegan wonders.

"Yeah... but that's also kind of a popular order for a lot of the gays here for some reason," the man dismisses.

"Um... I recognize that keychain... I know

someone who has a similar one. What did you say your name was?"

"I didn't!"

Aegan leaves... afraid of his own intuition.

"Hey, Roman... sorry your pizza took so long to make. We had an online delivery rush order."

The cashier brings him his food.

"Who was that guy?"

She shrugs.

"I've been here for two years, never seen him before."

* * * * *

It's been a long day. Various playdates and parties pulled the family away from the house, but their minds were always on Aegan being back home... and they bragged to their friends, online and offline, about it. The house returns to quiet as the younger Washingtons are now long lost to slumber from a day of joy.

Aegan sits on his bed, staring at his memorabilia... slightly bothered that things are out of place. It's been years, though... the audacity to expect it to remain unchanged. Hannon's items are scattered throughout the house, but this room is Aegan's in more ways than one. He pulls his collection from under his bed... noticing the finger prints and dig marks on the cover of one of his books... he ignores it to peruse the athletic cards in his possession... his back towards the door as Morocco stares at him.

He turns a few more pages, pretending to be unaware... Morocco eases away from the door.

"You may as well come on in," Aegan offers.

"You beat that guy up in Boystown, didn't you?"

Aegan turns a few pages...

"Why didn't you?"

"You were never supposed to leave, Aegan."

"There's a lot about me you will never understand or know. There's a reason I am the way I am... and I am glad you don't have to know about that."

"That's not fair, Aegan."

"Life's not fair. I took my journals with me for a reason. Y'all don't need to know everything about me. Y'all weren't going to grow if I stayed... and I needed ya'll to grow."

"None of us are fighters, Aegan. Where did you get that from?"

"There's a reason I am at Berkeley... I like to leave my mark in places impossible. But I also wanted to live in a world of people who think like I do... if even for just a moment. Chicago will always be home, but I learned a lot from when we lived in Cali. I still keep in touch with a lot of my elementary school buds... and it is great to reunite with them. We used to love to challenge everything... our curiosity made us smart. The more we learned, the more we fought back. And then, when I'm old enough to appreciate Hanjoon... it all made sense."

"Eigan's Hanjoon?"

"Yup."

Morocco has been given a glimpse into a world that no one knows exists.

"I'm sorry I scratched the cover of your book," Morocco lowers his head.

"Aa... you just acting out because you think I abandoned you. I left you because you are stronger than you give yourself credit... but you never needed to put your strength in action. That's why you feel so ashamed right now... and for whatever reason, you needed that reminder. Hanjoon's murder hit me in a way... and I am still learning a few things. One of which is to let life give me joys... whether or not I keep them secret is on me... but I should enjoy them. People respect you because of me... which is fine. But you forget that you are worthy of respect simply because you exist. In today's climate... you need to learn that more than ever. I definitely won't be able to make these trips when Ivey Joon is born–"

"WHAT!?"

Denae walks up at the wrong time. 'Goddamnit, I stay in trouble in this house.' Like his dad in more ways than one.

Aegan stays silent.

"And you're naming him after both..."

Denae begins to cry a little.

"Ma... stop!!!" Aegan groans.

"I can't help it!"

Denae's tears bring Marcus upstairs.

She embraces his neck... and he picks her up.

"What's wrong? What did you do to your mother?"

"I'M ABOUT TO BE A GUNCLE!" Morocco yells.

"When does the RV get here? We need to hit the road in a bit!"

Marcus checks his watch, on the phone with the family's assistant. He's not even concerned about whatever Lamar and Morocco are doing wherever in the house. No sense in even pretending anymore, as...

"that son of yours keeps getting bolder."

Denae rolls her eyes.

"Well, wherever he is, he is not upstairs."

Hyun and his two friends, Jeremy and Winston, are making a bit of a ruckus in the main room off the kitchen. Jeremy constantly texting and keeping some girl updated; Winston and Hyun laughing about some secret joke that apparently only those two understand. It's a different kind of commotion in the house... but still rowdy boys being boys.

Marcus smiles. There's a continuity here, Hyun is well established; Bassel; Jermaine; Artemis; Apollo... no assassinations to worry about... no moves for careers to unsettle the norm. It's a stability that will serve these sons well.

Hyun's phone rings...

"No, Cierra... you cannot come! I already told you that! Leave me alone!"

A girl cries on speaker phone, as Hyun puts the call on mute to laugh with Winston again.

"Hyun, go find your brother?"

Marcus needs a little quiet. Hyun returns to his phone.

"I gotta go, my dad needs me. Stop calling my phone: it's been over!"

He gets up to go find Morocco.

"You need any help, Mrs. Washington?"

Winston tries to snuggle up to Denae, in the absence of Hyun.

"Boy, go sit yourself down somewhere," she shoos him away.

He laughs and goes back to the sectional.

Hyun finds Morocco and Lamar in the study...

"Ugh, this house is too small," Morocco groans.

"I'm telling mom," Hyun turns to run upstairs.

"How you going to betray the code... that's fucked up!"

Morocco adjusts himself, as Lamar just observes the interaction.

"Buy me that new racing game I've been begging you for... and I'll keep quiet," Hyun Blackmails Morocco.

"That's not how this works!"

Morocco prepares to charge his brother.

"MOOOM!" Hyun backs away. "Lamar, get your boyfriend!"

Denae comes downstairs...

"I need you to help with the babies."

She commands, without coming around the corner. Morocco and Lamar get up to start packing for the younger siblings.

"Is Hannon coming?"

"No, his plane lands the day we arrive down there. And Aegan gets there the day after."

Denae heads back upstairs.

"Aegan's coming!?"

Hyun practically cheers; Bassel also brightens up, listening from the pool table. Even though Hannon is the oldest, Aegan is the legend in the family. In fact, the younger siblings remain confused on who is actually older.

"The RV will be here in a bit," Marcus shouts.

The boys begin to gather their stuff... this is going to be a LONG ride, but part of this is about the bonding, not just the destination.

Denae's brothers and Marcus used to go fishing every year; and for almost a decade, they've extended the invitation to their respective sons. This is Hyun's first time going out on the boat, and he is bringing his friends along. Morocco went one time, but fishing isn't really his thing. Since he and Lamar are going steady, this will also be his first time on the trip. Morocco will stay with his youngest brothers and the women... going shopping, making a fuss at the restaurant, going to a few shows. That's what he is looking forward to.

Denae and Marcus used to take this journey a few times in college, but this is the first time in adulthood. On the road, the kids marvel at the countryside; it's nice to have them along for the ride.

"I don't get it, Morocco, why doesn't she understand I am not trying to be tied down right now?"

"Do you like her?" Morocco asks for the nth time.

"Not like that, I got too many girls to choose from... why settle? She not even a baddie," Hyun rejects.

"Then why you even bother?" Morocco

chastises.

"Hey, attention is attention!"

Hyun and his two friends laugh. Morocco rolls his eyes.

"Don't get caught up, these girls crazy these days–" Morocco warns.

"So are the boys," Hyun teases his brother.

"That's why I'm sticking to one!"

Morocco is now the default for the family. Over the past few years, especially with Aegan being in college, he has tried to pass on what wisdom he can. Hyun kind of operates the way Morocco imagines Aegan would have... just a lot more friendly, and a lot less purpose in life right now. He's just a normal kid going through normal stuff... chasing his brother's legacy. He overhears the three talking about some of the plaques in school.

"You're not going to beat his record," Jeremy, not looking up from sexting with his girl.

"I was just close... like right there! I got way more poaches though."

Hyun tosses his rugby ball in the air, as they sit and watch a movie while the RV glides down I-55.

"And more penalties! Aegan never had to worry about poaching much, though... their offense was unstoppable, and their forwards were stout!" Winston reminds him.

"I'm still good at what I do... wing or flanker... If I go wing all next year, Aegan's record is gone!" Hyun believes, more than reality will confirm.

Morocco understands why Hyun feels it necessary to chase Aegan. There's not as much pressure in finding identity and chasing legacy. Hyun is solidly, authentically himself. He begged to go to The Academy. Morocco doesn't feel disrespected; he has a legacy at Sable that none of his brothers will be able to overshadow. Lamar is overwhelmed by the greatness the Washingtons attempt to live by. He almost understands some of the pressure that Morocco wanted to avoid.

"No wonder you went to Sable... everyone in your family is competitive," Lamar remarks.

For whatever reason, it doesn't hit Morocco properly... intent notwithstanding.

"I went to Sable to form my own competition," he corrects.

Lamar rubs his back... but it feels patronizing.

On a stop in Mehlville, Missouri; Morocco and Lamar, walking with Artemis and Apollo...

"Man, we look so gay right now!"

Lamar squirms a bit.

"Um... we are gay. Fuck you mean?"

Morocco is a little annoyed with this continued discussion.

"So... you're completely fine with us being in strange places looking like this?"

"Yes, Lamar, I love you... why wouldn't I want to show that off to the world!"

Lamar tries to get out of his discomfort...

"We've been doing this for a few years now, Morocco... we about ready to make the next step, I guess. We've never really traveled like this before... it just feels right. It feels natural. Maybe we should start planning a wedding," Lamar offers.

"Not if this is your idea of a proposal," Morocco laughs. "But, I'd say yes... and you already know that."

They kiss... ignoring a few jeers from strangers.

That makes an impression on Morocco. Being out in public away from home... and Lamar appears to have finally found his strength.

Social media posts announce Lamar and Morocco's wedding, showing a picture of them kissing outside the mall. Recently graduated Sable alumni across the country make plans to see them finally tie the knot. Many of them have been waiting on this for a few years, one of the first weddings of the most recent Sable graduating class. They all know what it took for them to finally choose each other. Lamar is the only one for Morocco, and Morocco for Lamar.

* * * * *

Mother Marlon stands on the front porch, watching the large RV pull up to their home.

"Must be someone famous."

Mr. Marlon waves from his chair, copying his wife.

"That's Denae and Marcus with the kids, Remy."

Mother Washington pours him a glass of lemonade:

perfect for the hot, Nawlins July. And plenty on standby for this hoard about to ascend.

"The kids... what kids? They always drive down with Eigan... that's only one kid."

Mr. Marlon scratches his head, fumbling for the glass... needing both hands to hold it.

"Nyah... too sweet!"

Mr. Marlon stares at the glass cautiously, not wanting to sip.

"Ain't no sugar in there," Mother Marlon lies.

"Then it's just right," he sips... then gulps the cool drink.

The kids run up to the porch, ignoring their bags to hug the grandparents; Artemis and Apollo trailing.

"Hmmm... them two look different... Hannon... who's that? Morocco or Eigan. Why they so short? Denae, why you not feeding them?!"

Mr. Marlon hugs his grandsons... and the two friends of Hyun.

"That's Jeremy and that's Winston," he introduces.

"Does Marcus know?" A puzzled look grows on Mr. Marlon's face.

"Oh, dad... these two are Hyun's friends from school."

Denae rolls her eyes, recognizing some of her dad's humor is still there.

"They not going on the boat, are they? Who gon' keep me company on the pier?"

Mr Marlon misses not being able to go out on the water anymore; the doctors recommend he not even go on the pier this year, since it's such heat this summer.

Coming up the block... a father, holding his son, walks with a woman, who appears to be expecting. Mother Marlon gasps... Mr. Marlon sees what she's staring at...

"Look at Marcus... who that with him?"

"Remy, that's Aegan," Mother Marlon corrects.

"In her belly? I know what my daughter looks like, Anna!"

He struggles with recognizing them; but Mr. Marlon radiates at seeing the three, nonetheless.

"Hey grampa, this is your great-grandson."

Aegan relieves all confusion.

Mr. Marlon pauses... then cries..."And life goes on..." as he says every time he meets a new extension of the family.

"Give me that boy! Aegan, you still beating Hannon at everything."

"He's about to have a sibling, we don't want to know if it's a boy or girl just yet," Kendra extends her hand.

"It's good to see you again..."

Mr. Marlon stares at the baby.

"He almost looks like Mario."

The three spend some time on the front porch with

Mr. Marlon, as Denae and her mother cackle and laugh just inside the door. She pulls her daughter back, heading towards the kitchen.

"Today is a really good day for him, he rattled off all the grandkids' names because he wanted to be sure to get them right," Mother Marlon tells Denae, Morocco listening earnestly.

Aegan, with his secrets again, got in town a bit early... and with, 'I guess, the girl he's dating. Why didn't he tell me?'

"Gram-ma, I'm going to go lay down."

The trip wore him out just a bit.

"Lamar stays down here, young man," Mother Marlon reminds him.

* * * * * *

Morocco wakes up... the house is deceptively quiet. He goes downstairs: Bassel is in the kitchen preparing a meal with his grandmother's orders... the house cook mainly handles the prep. Mother Marlon will serve for her family today.

"The Parkers eating with us?"

She was surprised they made the trip down, since she hadn't seen them in a while. Joey and Hannon still as inseparable as they have always been.

"They're not going to pass on your cooking, mom. Eating at the restaurant is for guests, not family,"

Denae watches Bassel, "careful with the knives." Morocco enters the kitchen.

"Where is everyone?"

He sees his grandfather, slightly reclined, holding Ivey Joon; the baby's mother sitting next to them, watching TV.

"Everyone's in town; so they took a boat out today, it's nice enough. The boys are exploring the park... the twins are asleep. Shopping or a show?" Denae offers.

Aegan, needing a little escape from his newborn, always finds his own corner of the boat away from everyone; away from the discussions; in company with his own thoughts... and many times, the best catch. Hyun and his friends are close enough to be heard, but not annoying.

Lamar seeks a moment with Aegan.

"I want to marry your brother."

Almost as bold as the day he first talked to Aegan about having feelings for Morocco...

"Except you sound very sure of yourself, today... and that's a good sign. He's not going to want something big, so be careful with that. You know I'm going to tell him—"

"I already asked him," Lamar beams. "He said yes. But I know how much he values you."

"I don't have any opinion on your relationship. I don't hold you accountable for anything he says about you, because it is none of my business. So the only blessing you need... is his. Not even my parents. And if they have a problem, I can head them off at the pass. He's going to be the first one to have a wedding.

So, there... now he can hang a milestone over us," Aegan laughs, slightly lying.

He has a few issues with Lamar, but Morocco pretends to be happy. Their relationship seems standard... on auto-pilot. It just is. But it also doesn't seem like the type of guy Morocco would date. To be fair, he did spend a few years away at college getting the chance to find himself; maybe Morocco changed as well. Something about that guy in the pizza parlor... but that would be a violation of trust. 'Even if he had dated Morocco at some point,' Aegan is no matchmaker. "People are allowed to change," as he reminds himself of his own journey.

Everyone of Mr. Marlon's grandchildren have fallen asleep in his arms at one point or another in their life. And now... another great-gran... this time from his baby girl, now a grandma herself. He remembers he met Anna in college... and used to bounce Mario on his knee. Youngins have to be pried from his hands.

He wakes up...

"Anna... come get the baby!"

Said softly, with calm urgency. She heard him, nonetheless, dropping the dish she was cleaning...

An emergency call comes over the boat's radio...

Marcus sits in the hallway, flanked by two of his oldest sons. His wife and her three brothers are in one room... his second-oldest son is down the hall, now by himself. Marcus holds his grandchild... these four being the only Washingtons in a crowd of Marlons.

"Life goes on..."

He just keeps murmuring to himself, as he refuses to cry; and almost gets mad at his sons if one of them tries to tear up. None of his in-laws are crying... it would be disrespectful. Even Mother Marlon is quiet right now.

The family postpones a formal announcement; but thanks to some nurse, whose life did benefit from the man hooked to machines in the room, news cameras are waiting outside the hospital.

Nothing malicious, but... damn.

Phones across Louisiana receive breaking news banners... this is a huge statewide story, and because of Denae's broadcast career, fans across the nation will find out soon. Attempts to call her work phone go unnoticed: she left it in Chicago.

Marcus stares across the hall, blank.

"How's your brother?"

No one answers.

The elevator dings...

"Kendra Washington?"

They hear a man's voice say. The family looks at each other. 'Are there two Kendras on this floor?'

A nurse takes the strange man up the hall... to the

room where... Aegan is? And closes the door behind him.

The elevator dings again...

"Ma, what are you doing here? You shouldn't be traveling," Marcus scolds.

She ignores her son and scooches him and his sons out the way so she can sit down.

"Julian called me from the airport... he was on his way to New Zealand, but came here first. Who's watching Hyun and them?"

"Who the hell is Julian?" the three men murmur.

Two tragedies in one day: one of nature, as it was just time... one of bigotry and legality, as doctors refuse to treat Kendra in need of an emergency procedure with her uterus...

The family gives Aegan his space, because they know he processes differently. Even for those who try, he uncomfortably entertains their presence, and they leave. Aegan and Julian stay at the hospital: visiting hours don't apply to some people... and Aegan accepts a third tragedy later in the week.

It's quieter in the home. Save Morocco and Lamar, Hannon has taken the rest of the kids back to Chicago by flight, calling the nanny back into duty a little earlier than expected.

"That's a lot to take in," Lamar, allowed to sleep in the same room as Morocco.

"That's my brother... he's impenetrable. I wish I got to know her."

Morocco holds his nephew, taking a lot in about how his brother handles life. Aegan is still in Nawlins, but feels farther away than ever.

Undecided on what path to take, Morocco signs up for physiology credits at a community college in Chicago, while Lamar completes his studies at the university in Hyde Park that put the academic world on notice. Lamar and Morocco, finally living together without fear of curfews, endure the trappings of couple-hood.

The country buzzes over a new series on the streaming services. It centers around some gay couple and hockey players. Both Morocco and Lamar are underwhelmed by the spectacle. Neither are interested in the same old 'white closeted gays fall in love but are too scared to be open about it, in spite of being protected by their whiteness' trope that has been repeated in gay-centered movies for decades.

"I'm not going to any watch party, that series is not on my purview."

Lamar declines the invitation to Daddy Halsted's for this week's episode, but something in the universe tells Morocco he should go. It's going to be a social night, so a few of their friends from prep school and other gays they have met around the community will be in the restaurant; former athletes, including some hockey players from Sable, obviously. This one guy always has to have his camera out, videotaping everyone's response during the episodes.

Morocco ignores it.

All of a sudden... on the screen... everyone is watching the hockey finals... one of the gay guy's teams wins it all... 'surprise surprise.' Then, he has a moment where he looks into the stands...

Morocco's eyes widen, anticipation in the restaurant... for what's about to happen on the screen.

"Oh my goodness..."

as phones come out so people can record their own reactions, no consent from nor concern of those who might not want to be on video.

As the kiss on the ice happens... the restaurant explodes in cheers and jubilation, claps and gasps... but the scene isn't over... so

"SHHHHHH!!"

One head bowed in reflection goes unnoticed by the crowd.

A little downtime in Annapolis, whatever that looks like... and a few men in the dorms look at reaction videos from the new streaming series, as the latest episode featured one of the hockey players coming out of the closet. Roman isn't interested in watching the program, but he's been wary of the reception, since being gay is under attack in the US.

This series has given the country a chance to talk about uncomfortable topics, and given a few gays a lot of courage about being authentic. A few gays from Chicago had just been chatting about the upcoming nuptials for Morocco and Lamar, which Roman gives a cautious smile while listening.

"Look on Loren's page," one of the guys from Sable recommends, and they all crowd his phone, including Roman, also curious... uncharacteristically.

"I think this is the scene where he outs himself on the ice," Martin narrates.

Raised arms cover most of the video as the room cheers and gasps... but Roman has become fixated on a now bowed head... it's the only thing he can see in the video.

He pauses... looks up... then quietly retreats from the common space.

"I love him, Aegan."

Morocco lays in bed, not concerned about the time difference between Chicago and Berkeley, as Aegan was in the middle of good, and necessary sleep. His son wrenches next to him.

"And yet, you are on the phone with me right now... you brought this topic up!"

Aegan yawns, muffling the phone from his snores. Morocco knows he is half-asleep, but still.

"I want this, more than anything in the world," Morocco reasons.

"Take me off speaker! Who are you really thinking about, though?" Aegan groans.

"Lamar! And you don't pay this phone bill," Morocco yells.

"Whatever, Morocco. Remember when you had that crush back in elementary school. And you struggled trying to tell me you like a boy instead of a girl? I always known you like dick."

"Shut the fuck up, Aegan!"

"Man... I didn't mean it like that. My point is... I know you better than you think I do. Lamar represents something different for you. He's your first exploration. But, suppose he was just your prep for something better?"

"You've been gone too long to think you know me," Morocco corrects.

"You're still fundamentally the same person. You like what you like. You liked that little boy back then because he beat up all the kids on the playground. You like guys who are sure of themselves. Lamar ever been that?"

"YES! You never met him, get the fuck outta my business, Aegan–"

Denae peeks in.

"HEY, You trying to wake up the WHOLE house? What time is it in California, anyway? Let that man sleep!"

"I'm good, ma. All he gon' do is call me back as soon as you leave."

Aegan yawns again.

"All I'm going to say is this... you can change who you date... you can change who you marry... you can't change who makes your heart beat. Morocco... you always make my heart beat, man. I love you. And you know I got your back either way."

Morocco sits quiet on the phone... Denae sees it in his face. Marcus makes her heart beat... she makes Marcus' heart beat.

"He needs to marry you to make himself feel good... 'bout like other people who need to remain nameless."

Aegan thinks about a late former senator elected by the state of Georgia, who had red-hair... and a fiery, baritone voice.

"And that's not a bad thing, Aegan. Gay men are allowed to feel good about each other!"

Morocco ends the call. Denae slowly turns...

"I have loved him since I met him, ma. Aegan

was there. Hannon was there. Joey was there. They saw it. It's always been Lamar for me."

Denae tilts her head... and walks off to grab the morning paper.

A holiday wedding... as Lamar doesn't want to go into another year without Morocco legally by his side. The doors to the sanctuary are closed, as sweaty palms grind against each other. One man prepares to take a chance on another... two hearts race towards one another.

"Is there anyone here who has any reason why these two should not be wed... speak now, or forever hold your peace."

Lamar turns, gazing back at the audience; pretending to prepare to outman any potential objectors. The crowd giggles and murmurs.

Morocco's heart pauses... skips a beat... there's a presence in the air.

He looks up, seemingly the only one who can hear commotion at the front of the building... as ushers fail to hold the doors closed...

"MOROCCO!"

The crowd turns to see who would dare upset this ceremony.

Lamar turns to Morocco, surprised, as he is staring at the foyer...

He recognizes the voice... and takes a step towards the door.

"What are you doing?" Lamar whispers.

"I have to..."

Morocco finds confidence in his words.

"It was always supposed to be him."

He leaves the altar... as the strange man fully enters the church... resplendent in his Navy Dress whites...

strange to everyone... but to the only one that matters... recognizable!

Roman opens his arms, and Morocco jumps in.

"I should have never let you walk away. I just didn't know what to do... but I know I want you. Whatever comes with that. I know I can survive... and I know I can thrive without you. But I don't want to."

Morocco kisses him...

"It wasn't your fault. I didn't want you to be the person I absolutely want to spend my life with. I know that doesn't make sense... and I made that mistake once: it won't happen again."

The two exit the church. The congregation, silently, turns to the front... demanding answers.

"I came out to my whole family... for this?!"

Lamar weathered the phone calls and the social media posts, Bible verses; political stances... for weeks, months even... once invitations started going out.

Having seen this relationship from the beginning... Dr. Barnes is a bit relieved. She'll console her son; but still wants him to find a man he actually likes, not someone who makes him feel acceptable.

Aegan leaves the altar, heading out the back.

"Where are you going?" Marcus objects.

Aegan stops, turns... looks at his dad as if he asked the dumbest question in the world...

"They're going to need a witness in order to

get married."

Aegan turns back around... takes Ivey Joon from a cousin... and exits the church.

"Them two right there..."

Denae and Mother Washington giggle... then gather their stuff.

Mother Marlon is tired of fussing in the kitchen.

"I wouldn't do it that way!"

She observes, while tasting the food. For a new adventure in life, Denae takes over running her mother's restaurant, as retirement looms for Mother Marlon with the passing of her husband. Denae handles the recipes... Mario handles the receipts, his finance degree works for the family now. Bassel has abandoned his love of sports to take up culinary, hoping to carry on a strong family tradition in cooking, combining lessons learned from both sides of his family. He wants to send Hyun off to "Dear, Old U" with a fantastic meal.

On their way to the restaurant... or at least should have been some time ago...

"You not gon' get that boy ready? It's past time to go!"

Marcus chastises Aegan for letting Ivey Joon run around naked.

"Let my son alone!"

Aegan defends... as Morocco playfully chases the child, encouraging the disorder. Ivey Joon squeals with delight, slightly aware that his grandfather is annoyed.

"I hope you're more organized when you get to New Zealand. The Eagles may accept this, but not them Kiwis. How you gon' be a scrummy for grown men, and this little boy can run you?"

Marcus looks at his watch.

"That's MY son," Aegan puffs.

Marcus forgets that Aegan is a fantastic scrum-half BECAUSE of his ability to assess people and predict outcomes.

Roman glows... he still cannot believe that Morocco loves him... and that he is allowed to love such a special man. They have an early flight to Panama, as they begin their life together.

Marcus sits with him.

"Linguistics and diplomacy, huh? Maybe you can do something about some of this current foolishness?"

"Nah... I'm doing my commitment, then Morocco and I will figure it out. He'll be done with his credits next year, and we'll definitely be back for his graduation, when he 'takes tomorrow, boldy.' I can't wait to see him in a cap and gown. He's already got so much lined up: HIV education; working with a few dance teams; the baseball league starts in November down there..."

Roman downplays his own graduation from the
Naval Academy, and future career.
Marcus looks at Aegan... then at Roman... and
nods his head in agreement.

Sometimes life prepares you for the partner you're
supposed to have... the life you're supposed to
lead.

Ivey Joon plops down on his grandfather.

"Now, we can go," Aegan stands.

Thank you

www.ingramcontent.com/pod-product-compliance
Lightning Source LLC
Chambersburg PA
CBHW012039140726
47991CB00011B/3206